"Caramellina," Rafaele murmured again, lost in the warm depths of her gaze and the soft feel of her skin beneath his fingers. "You even smell sweet." A combination of roses and vanilla and something he wasn't quite sure of but it was intoxicating.

He stared into her luminous eyes for a long time. And for every moment of it she met his gaze. They stood, stilled in that silent connection until he saw it—that sensual curiosity that he felt, revealed and reflected in her. More than curiosity, it was a pull that could no longer be ignored. Gracie's lips parted and the smallest of sighs escaped her.

"Just kiss me already."

He brushed his lips over hers as gently as he was able, desperately trying to go slow. To seduce. Because he knew she was flighty. He'd pull out every trick he knew to tempt her closer, so she wouldn't startle and step back. He wanted this too much.

Natalie Anderson adores a happy ending—which is why she always reads the back of a book first. Just to be sure. So you can be certain you've got a happy ending in your hands right now—because she promises nothing less. Along with happy endings, she loves peppermint-filled dark chocolate, pineapple juice and extremely long showers. Not to mention spending hours teasing her imaginary friends with dating dilemmas. She tends to torment them before eventually relenting and offering—you guessed it—a happy ending. She lives in Christchurch, New Zealand, with her gorgeous husband and four fabulous children.

If, like her, you love a happy ending, be sure to come say hi at Facebook.com/authornataliea, follow @authornataliea on Twitter or visit her website/blog, natalie-anderson.com.

Books by Natalie Anderson

Harlequin Presents

Claiming His Convenient Fiancée
The Forgotten Gallo Bride
The King's Captive Virgin

One Night With Consequences

Princess's Pregnancy Secret

The Throne of San Felipe

The Secret That Shocked De Santis
The Mistress That Tamed De Santis

Natalie Anderson

AWAKENING HIS INNOCENT CINDERELLA

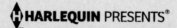

HARLEQUIN PRESENTS®

Recycling programs
for this product may
not exist in your area.

ISBN-13: 978-1-335-53800-0

Awakening His Innocent Cinderella

First North American publication 2018

Copyright © 2018 by Natalie Anderson

Printed in U.S.A.

AWAKENING HIS INNOCENT CINDERELLA

For Bridge and Kat—thank you so much for the coffee catch-ups, giggles and goss. Thursdays are the best!

CHAPTER ONE

BRUSHING BACK A lock of hair, Gracie James entered the last three digits into the discreet keypad and paused expectantly. An electronic beep sounded and the heavy iron gates smoothly swung back. She wheeled her bike through the opening and leaned it against the nearest of the tall trees that formed a guard of honour the length of the driveway. She walked the rest of the way, making the most of her opportunity to see one of Lake Como's luxury hideaways and cooling down from her ride at the same time. The grounds were stunning enough, but she still gasped when the building came into view.

Oh…yes.

In the gorgeous Italian village of Bellezzo, where she'd been living for the last four months, Gracie had thought she'd become immune to the stunning architecture Italy had to offer. So wrong. Villa Rosetta was an eighteenth-century masterpiece of symmetry and style with its precisely spaced archways, three floors of warm-coloured stone with large, gleaming windows and that perfectly placed turret on top. The luxury looked all the more magical thanks to the golden hue from the setting sun.

'Amazing,' she whispered as she walked to the edge of the marble patio to get a better look. 'Amazing, amazing, amazing.'

The villa had long been an exclusive holiday home for wealthy families seeking privacy and luxury during the Italian summer, but for the last month it had been closed. Apparently the new owner had undertaken refurbishment work—upsetting the locals by shutting off access and shipping in city contractors.

No one in Bellezzo knew what he had planned now the work had been completed. But Gracie had heard whispers that he might not lease it out any more, which worried the villagers—the spending power of the beautiful people was of huge benefit to the community. Now, according to one gossip, Rafael Vitale, billionaire broker and reckless playboy, planned to have orgies there. Gracie inwardly giggled at the ridiculous thought—though the villa was certainly armed with all the privacy required for decadence and sinful delight.

Not that she knew much about either. But it didn't seem right to her that just one person would enjoy this. She'd feel like a peanut rattling around in a shoebox if she lived here alone. So, yes, bring on the nymphs and satyrs.

She glanced along the villa's private beach and saw the narrow hidden channel behind the wall through which boats could reach the lavish boat shed. She turned to the gardens—the reason for her visit. On the first terrace a swimming pool and a spa were set into crisply manicured lawns, with a half-dozen sun loungers evenly placed along the side. The azure water was another temptation—no one would ever know if she had a quick, secret dip. She glanced at her watch and reluctantly walked past to that springy, lush lawn.

Hidden beyond the trimmed hedges up on the next terrace was the famous tangled rose garden—dozens of heirloom roses planted in a deceptively 'careless' manner that formed a sweet-scented lover's knot—entrancing and romantic and utterly gorgeous. No wonder her elderly neighbour Alex Peterson had been desperate for her to check on them.

She'd met the widower on her first day in Bellezzo. He lived on the ground floor of the small apartment building in which she'd rented a small unit. She'd stopped to enjoy the roses growing in the container garden by the gate. They'd started talking—in English—a heavenly treat given her appalling Italian.

Like her, Alex was an import. He'd married an Italian woman and had lived lakeside with her for fifty years until her death eleven months ago. His son lived in Milan, while his daughter and grandchildren lived in London. His life now was all about his hybrid roses as he aimed to create delicately scented flowers with masses of petals, while at the same time avoiding the matchmaking attempts of half the village.

It had become Gracie's habit to bring him a pastry in her afternoon break from the café where she worked—Bar Pasticceria Zullo. But he'd been knocked down with the flu in the height of summer, which was unfair, and given his age she was worried. In turn, he was overly agitated about the precious flowers that he'd been tending for decades.

Despite the villa's sale, Alex had refused to relinquish responsibility for the rose garden. Seeing it in full bloom now, she wasn't surprised. With the amount of work that he'd put in, she knew he wanted them perfect for the new owner. He'd been desperate for her to ensure they weren't wilting in the intense heat. Even now, at nightfall, the temperature was a touch too hot.

Tucking that loose strand of hair back again, Gracie fossicked for the hose and spent five minutes figuring out how to attach the thing to the tap. Natural gardener she was not. But finally she got it sorted. Then she phoned her friend because she'd already taken longer than planned.

'Alex, it's me, Gracie. I'm at the villa. The roses are beautiful. I'll just water them and come back.'

'How are they looking?'

'Amazing. I'll take a picture for you.'

'Don't worry about bringing me a picture. You just go into the village.'

She smiled at his bossiness. 'I'm not leaving you alone for any longer than necessary. You're not well.'

'I'm not alone. Sofia arrived ten minutes ago with six pints of minestrone and won't leave until I've eaten it all. I don't know why she's fussing. I'm not that sick.'

Sofia was the cousin of Francesca, Gracie's boss at the *pasticceria*, and she was formidable. 'Hide some in the roses.' Gracie laughed.

Her stomach rumbled in outrage, reminding her she'd not eaten since grabbing a small roll before the rush had begun. Six pints of Sofia's minestrone sounded fantastic to her.

'Are you crazy?' Alex muttered.

Gracie laughed again. 'I'll still—'

'Go into the village,' he interrupted. 'Enjoy the festival. It's your first. The fireworks are good.'

Gracie hesitated. She would like to go to the festival, especially seeing she'd spent all day baking a million pastries to be sold at the *pasticceria*'s stall, and Francesca had insisted she not work the evening shift in return. But Gracie was conscious of how horrible it was to be alone—especially when sick. 'Are you sure?'

'Of course I'm sure.' He sighed. 'Sofia has settled in. I won't get rid of her for ages.'

'Well, I'll check on you in the morning.'

'Not too early,' he said gruffly. 'You get up even earlier than I do.'

Gracie winced. Such were the perils of working both the early morning and the evening shifts at Bar Pasticceria Zullo, but working this hard to gain respect and a foothold was worth it, and she was happier than she'd ever been. 'I'll see you after my first shift, then.'

'I look forward to it. Thank you, Gracie.'

'My pleasure, Alex.'

Happy that he sounded so much better, she quickly snapped a picture to show him in the morning anyway. As soon as she got to the village she would be visiting the *pasticceria* for some sustenance. Tonight was Bellezzo's annual festival—featuring lanterns on the lake, music and dancing. Fireworks. Food. Families. *Fun.* All the things she'd never experienced.

There'd be tourists, of course, plenty of tourists, but Gracie refused to consider herself one. She was a local with a home and she was determined to remain. After a childhood of upheaval and constantly having to rebuild, her spirits soared at the pleasure of now having a place to call hers. And while she might not have family here, she had a friend who *needed* her. She loved that.

Finally she flicked on the hose. The power of it caught her unawares. With a laugh she gripped it more tightly, giving each rose bush a big drink.

A hand suddenly slammed on her shoulder from behind—hard and heavy and so unexpected she screamed and whirled, brandishing the hose like a machine gun. All she could make out in the blurry spray was a massively large masculine frame and that simply made her aim all the more accurate.

'What are you doing?' she shrieked at him.

'What are you doing?' he shouted back—matching her English—but his accent had an American tang.

He wrenched the hose from her but it twisted as he grabbed it, spraying a shockingly cold streak across her stomach before he flung it to the ground, the water gushing harmlessly across the lawn. Gasping, Gracie stared at her assailant.

He was stunning. Wet. Angry. Soaked to the skin, the tuxedo he was wearing was now ruined. *Tuxedo.* Her stunned feeble brain attempted some computations.

'Why the water cannon?' He wiped one hand over his face, the other down his front. Droplets of water splattered from his fingers.

That tux was saturated and this was no intruder. Instinctively—unthinkingly—she reached out to help sweep the streaming rivers of water from his suit. She brushed frantically, her hands sopping, until she realised that he was no longer attempting to do the same thing. He was standing utterly still. She froze too, mortification finally sinking in.

Slowly—reluctantly—she glanced up. She encountered glittering eyes so brown they were almost black and they were fringed with unfairly long lashes. Of course he had lashes like those. Superlative, to match the rest of him. As for the cheekbones? You could slice steak on them they were so high and sharp and, *oh, goodness…*

'Sorry.' She whipped her hands behind her back and wished for another cold shock of water from that hose, because now she was so hot it was amazing her blouse wasn't steaming. She stared up at the masculine magnificence towering several inches above her. She knew who this was. Francesca had flashed her a picture printed in the local newsletter when she'd told her about the sale of the villa. Gracie hadn't understood a word of the accompanying text but that quick glimpse of those cheekbones had been unforgettable. Rafael Vitale. The billionaire orgy man himself.

'You're not supposed to be here,' she said shakily.

'I think that's my line. Again.' He watched her coolly, decidedly unimpressed. 'This is my house. You're the invader.'

'I'm so sorry.' She pulled on a smile and hoped he'd forgive her. 'Wasn't expecting you to be home.'

'Clearly not.' He didn't smile back. Definitely not seeing the funny side yet.

She was *dying*…and was…uh…*stunned.*

Rafael Vitale was so much more than anyone she'd ever met—more tall, more good looking, more well dressed, aside from—

'You're very wet. I'm so sorry.' She glanced at the water still streaming from his muscular frame and died all over again. 'Will it be…okay?'

'No,' he answered bluntly, and peeled off the sodden jacket.

Paralysed, Gracie stared, slack-jawed. His shirt was glued to his skin. *Glued.* She could see the ridges of his muscles—of which there were many. Hot, hard muscles. He was the most strapping man. Panty-dropping gorgeous but so intimidating that she actually giggled. He looked up from shaking out the jacket and shot her another less than impressed look.

She covered her mouth with her hand. She really needed to stop staring at him. But she couldn't. Was this what instant attraction felt like? Lust at first sight? She inwardly squirmed at her unruly overheated reaction. No wonder he was a rake if all women had this reaction to his appearance. He'd have his pick of bedmates. Clearly he thought she was a complete fool. But, then, he must be completely used to getting this kind of reaction, which meant she was as much of a fool as any of them. Hell, she needed to pull herself together!

Quickly she moved to get away from him but she slipped on the wet grass. Her feet slithered out from under her and she went down awkwardly, smashing her knee hard.

This time he slammed his strong hand beneath her elbow. Without any apparent effort he hauled her to her feet. Only, she slipped in her stupid wet sandals again. She heard a muttered curse and the next thing she knew she was pressed against his body as he formed a literal pillar of support. His arm was firmly about her waist, holding her far, far too close. Those muscles were even harder than they'd looked. And hotter.

Blistering with embarrassment, she couldn't bear to look up at him. Dimly she realised her knee was killing her, but her proximity to his physical perfection was providing the most amazing anaesthetic. The thought idly crossed her mind that his woodsy scent ought to be bottled and used in operations in every hospital theatre.

Another ferociously muttered curse made her blink.

'Are you all right?' he snapped.

He probably thought she was simple. Most definitely useless. She tried putting her weight on her foot and winced. A second later she was flying through the air into his arms. His arms, as she'd suspected, were very strong. And the chest she was now pressed against was very solid. Fortunately the contact kick-started her rational thinking processes.

'Put me down,' she said stiffly.

'And have you slip again and break your neck?' he snarled, stalking back towards the beautiful villa. 'You're a liability. Not just to yourself. The sooner you're off my property, the better.'

'You're going to carry me all the way to the gate?'

He probably was strong enough. She could feel his muscles burning through the cold, wet fabric. The man was *built*. But he was also obviously unimpressed. Desperately she suppressed her appreciative shiver. So inappropriate and lamely predictable. He must get women literally throwing themselves at him all the time. She was not going to be another. But as he effortlessly strode over the manicured lawns towards that magnificently impressive building, she couldn't hold in another giggle.

'Are you hysterical?'

She heard the unmistakable note of horror in his question.

'No.' She breathed in and steadied herself. 'I'm embarrassed. Laughing is my nervous release. I'm sorry.' She peered up to try to see into his face and braved another smile. 'At least it's better than crying.'

'Well, that's true,' he answered grimly. 'Heaven

forbid I have a tearful trespasser on my hands.' He climbed the wide steps and entered through the open doorway into the glorious large lounge. 'I'm Rafael Vitale.'

'I figured.'

'And you are?'

Now she was inside, it immediately struck her that the best way of minimising his insane effect on her was to scope out the amazing interior of the villa instead. But he didn't stop in the eye-poppingly ornate lounge, rather he marched straight through it down a long corridor to a vast kitchen. He unceremoniously set her on the large table. Fascinated, Gracie gaped at the gleaming appliances.

'Wow,' she murmured as she stared at the elegance of the set-up. 'State of the art.' And that was an understatement.

He gave the kitchen a dismissive glance and turned back to her with businesslike seriousness. 'Is it sore?'

'What?' Oh. Her knee. 'My embarrassment has numbed my knee.'

She snatched a breath and tried to look anywhere but at him again. Except he was so close and so good looking, her attention was the iron filing to his magnetism.

'How helpful,' he commented dryly. 'Ice will bring out the bruising.' He strode over to the gleaming fridge and pushed some buttons.

'Because I want a purple knee,' she muttered.

He didn't respond as he walked back, holding ice in a glass and a clean cloth.

'That's an impressive fridge. The whole place is impressive,' she babbled. 'This kitchen is bigger than our one at the bakery and that's a commercial operation. You could cook enough in here to feed an army. Though you'd *need* an army to use all the appliances at once.'

He still didn't respond, just neatly wrapped some ice in the cloth. She shivered before he got the cold pack anywhere near her, but at the same time was still sweltering with embarrassment. And awareness. And yet more embarrassment.

She stared hard at her lap as he bent before her.

'You're not supposed to be here.' She winced, desperately trying to ignore the brush of his fingers on her skin as he pushed up her skirt to reveal her grass-stained, bruised knee. 'The villa was supposed to be empty until tomorrow. That's what I heard.'

'You talk all the time when you're nervous too?' He held the ice to her knee.

'This isn't usual,' she muttered. Usually she went silent. She'd learned long ago that talking too much meant secrets might slip out and that habit was surprisingly hard to break. She preferred not to tell people about her upbringing now out of choice, rather than necessity. The difference of it made people awkward. 'You know, it's not that bad. You can stop with the ice now,' she gasped. 'I'm fine.'

He ignored her and increased the pressure even more. 'Here. Hold it firmly.'

Mortified at the realisation that the last thing the man wanted was to press an ice pack against her leg, she slapped her hand down to hold it in place, inadvertently hitting his hand in the process.

'Sorry,' she muttered, dying all over again. If she were a cat, she'd be down to her last life by now.

She pushed back a wet ribbon of hair and tried to ignore the fact that Rafael Vitale was unfastening his wet shirt. Ten timeless seconds later he wasn't wearing said shirt. Her mouth dried as her brain shorted out. His chest was bronzed and, as she'd suspected, his muscles were ultra-defined. Furthermore, he had the finest trail of hair leading to the waistband of his perfectly tailored black trousers. He was officially a living freaking angel. When he turned away, she quickly pressed the wrapped ice against her burning cheeks instead of her knee and racked her brains for what Francesca had told her about him.

Rafael Vitale had made billions from the kinds of financial transactions Gracie had no desire to ever understand and now he was amassing a property empire. Another thing she'd never understand.

She wanted only the one place to call home—that would make her happier than anything.

And if Francesca's favourite websites were to be believed, the guy dated models and aristocrats—as in the aristocrats who *were* models. He had an endless supply of stunning well-connected women to warm his bed. Seeing him in the flesh—indeed seeing most of his flesh—Gracie could totally understand why.

She pressed her legs together, primly rejecting the insidious warmth and restless kick deep within. The sooner she got away from here, the better. She'd embarrassed herself enough. She didn't need to drool over a man who was so far out of her league and who'd never send her a second look in ordinary circumstances. But his *kitchen* was totally droolworthy—she could make amazing things in this kitchen.

'Why did you take a photo?'

Startled, she glanced at him, registering the distance in his demeanour as he waited for her answer. She'd taken that snap *before* she'd started watering the roses, so for how long had he been watching her? 'I wanted to show him they were fine.'

'Show who what were fine?' He stepped closer.

She chose to focus on the smooth marble pastry bench on the opposite side from her and think about cold, cold things so she could speak without stuttering. 'Alex. The roses.'

'Who's Alex?'

'You don't know?' She glanced at Rafael again before remembering the searing impact on her senses.

'I assume he's a caretaker? This is my first visit to the villa,' he said briefly, his intense gaze not leaving her face.

Caretaker? The man had worked on this estate for the last forty years!

'You've not been here before?' She wrinkled her nose in confusion. 'Did you buy it without even seeing it and having that restoration work done?'

His lack of response confirmed it.

'Wow,' she muttered.

'This really is about the roses?'

'Of *course* it's about the roses. Why else would I be here?'

He didn't answer. She stared at him suspiciously. 'Did you think I was here to, what…hope to meet you?' The guy was unbearably arrogant.

She dragged her gaze back up from his chest to his eyes and didn't really blame him. But still.

'You wouldn't be the first woman to break into one of my properties.' A faintly amused look crossed his face as he regarded her damp blouse and skirt.

'I didn't break in,' she said spiritedly.

'Semantics.' He leaned back against the opposite bench, that hint of amusement making him even more fascinating. 'Mostly they try to find my bedroom.'

'I'm *not* a stalker.' At the thought of his bedroom her skin crisped.

'I'm relieved to hear it.' He angled his head and studied her.

Awareness rippled down Gracie's spine. She wasn't sure she trusted that new look in his eyes and she certainly didn't trust her own suddenly frantic pulse.

'You'd better go and get changed,' she said brightly, hoping he'd take the hint and cover up quickly. 'You obviously had somewhere to be and I need to get back to the village.' She wriggled forward to the edge of the table, preparing to put weight on her wretched knee.

'What's your name?'

His question was a perfectly innocuous, normal one, yet her heart thundered. She'd given so many variations as an answer to this in her childhood. For over a decade she'd not been able to tell anyone her real name. Lying, lying, lying.

It's for your safety, sweetheart. So we can stay together.

Hiding had meant constantly moving. She breathed in and shook off the whisper of the past. Now she'd chosen her own name—a family name too—so answering this question now shouldn't be stressful. Yet for a reason she couldn't quite identify, she didn't want to tell him.

For the first time, he actually smiled. It transformed him from moody fallen angel to silver screen hero in a heartbeat. There was no way she could answer him now. She couldn't actually speak.

'What does it matter?' he queried her reluctance with even more of a smile. 'You're never going to see me again.'

'Right. Right, of course… The thing is…' She bit her lip and decided to brave up. 'You're going to have to see me. I'm doing Alex's job for a few days.'

That smile vanished. 'Watering the roses?' he asked, for cold confirmation.

'Yes.'

'Use an automatic hydration system,' he snapped.

'They're like his babies,' she retorted scornfully. 'Would you use an automated feeding system for your babies?'

'Not an issue I ever plan to face.' He straightened to full height and put his hands on his hips, drawing her attention back to his sculpted, bare physique. 'Why are you doing his job?'

Gracie studied the floor tiles. 'He's unwell. He has the flu.'

'It's the height of summer—'

'He's older—'

'Should he still be working?'

'Of course he should.' She lifted her chin and glared at Rafael. The guy had no idea how lucky he was to have Alex working on his property.

'His judgement is impaired,' Rafael said coolly. 'He should never have given you the security code to get inside the gate.'

'He didn't want your precious flowers to frizzle in this heat. He was doing what he thought best.'

'All employees of this estate were under instruction to maintain security of the premises no matter what. Not to give the codes to just anyone.'

Gracie ignored the hit at being dismissed as 'just anyone'. 'He loves the roses. He's spent his *life* looking after those roses.'

'I don't care about the roses—'

'Clearly.' The man was an unfeeling jerk.

'I care about my privacy. And my security.'

'You don't want the common folk encroaching on your space? Or any rabid female stalkers lying in your bed?' She immediately wished she hadn't mentioned that as it put a disconcerting picture in her head.

'That's right.' He smiled. 'I don't wish to be bothered.'

'Well,' she said formally, 'if you'll just let me leave, then you won't be bothered any more. I'll be sure to check the roses when you're not here.'

'Too late,' he said softly, stepping forward so he was back in front of her. 'I'm already bothered.'

His tone put her on edge.

'Where are you from?' he asked. 'Why are you here?'

'I've already told you.'

'You've talked a lot but told me almost nothing.'

Ignoring the way he was standing too close, Gracie slid down from the kitchen table and gingerly tested her knee. To her relief, it wasn't too bad. 'Look, I'm fine. I'll get going now.'

'No.' He didn't walk any closer, but somehow seemed to block her escape route.

'Why not?' To avoid ogling his bare chest, she had no choice but to look up into his damnably handsome face.

A speculative light had entered his eyes. It was fascinating the way it warmed their colour.

'I'm late for the party,' he said. 'I'm going to need a good reason for why I'm so late.'

'Tell them the truth.' She shrugged. 'It's the easiest way.'

'You advise honesty?' His gaze narrowed on her.

'Always.' She made herself maintain eye contact despite the way just looking at him made her pulse skip like a schoolgirl's.

'You're always honest?'

Could he sound any more sardonic?

She folded her arms across her chest. 'Absolutely.'

He actually laughed. 'No one is ever absolutely honest.'

'Well, I am.' She'd vowed never to lie again. She'd had to do so far too much in the past.

'People lie all the time. For good reasons and for bad.' The corners of his mouth quirked up into that unbearably gorgeous smile. 'But seeing you're so good at being honest, you can come with me and tell them the truth.'

CHAPTER TWO

Gracie blinked at him, not sure she'd heard him correctly. 'I'm not coming with you.'

'It's at the Palazzo Chiara,' he added, as if she'd not spoken. 'Have you seen the *palazzo*? It makes this place look minuscule.'

She'd seen Palazzo Chiara from a tourist launch on the lake when she'd first arrived. The humongous estate had been converted into an exclusive luxury hotel. The playpen of real silver screen heroes and beyond wealthy sheiks and oligarchs who paid literally thousands of dollars to stay for just one night. Villa Rosetta was the *palazzo*'s 'little sister', though frankly Gracie thought the villa held more charm. Apparently she wasn't the only one—it was even harder to book a week here than a suite at the *palazzo*.

'I believe it has an amazing view of the fireworks and the lanterns,' he added softly.

She narrowed her eyes. He *had* listened in to her conversation with Alex. He'd been watching her for a while.

'I can see the fireworks from the village,' she said stiffly.

He might be the most handsome man she'd ever seen, but he had the inevitable flaw that came with such good looks and money—he was used to getting everything his own way. But this one time he wasn't getting it. Even if there was that secret part of her that wanted him to.

'You're a tourist. Don't you want to see what an elite party at a place like that is like?'

'Full of "elite" people such as your arrogant self?' she challenged bluntly. 'It doesn't sound all that.'

'None are as arrogant as I am.' His mouth curved and he put his hands on his hips.

Gracie narrowed her gaze. He was shameless at using his smile to his advantage. And his bare chest.

'Think of it as another experience for your travels,' he added.

She didn't bother correcting his assumption that she wasn't local. 'So I should feel grateful for the opportunity?'

'Most people would,' he said, apparently without a hint of irony.

'Unfortunately for you, I'm not most people,' she said haughtily. 'And I don't want any other "experience" with you either. My mother warned me about getting into cars with strangers.'

Literally *every* day of her childhood her mother had warned her. She'd been so afraid they'd be caught. That Gracie would be kidnapped and taken from her.

'But I'm no longer a stranger. You know who I am. I've even taken care of your bruised knee for you.'

'What I know gives me all the more reason to say no.'

His eyebrows shot up. 'Does my reputation precede me? What's the worst I could do?' His smile was so wicked. 'I don't think it would be *that* dreadful.'

The shift in him was like night from day. Suddenly he was charming and, darn it all, even more riveting. 'Why on earth do you want me going along with you?'

'Because it's going to be boring. Having you there might make it less so.'

So she was to be light relief for him? 'You want me to be your court jester? Or your pet Chihuahua?' She rolled her eyes. 'That's not going to be a thing.'

'Did you just refer to yourself as a dog?'

Her jaw dropped—then she snapped it shut. 'I have a job to finish here.'

'I think we both know your job here is done.'

'For today,' she said pointedly, lifting her chin. 'I promised Alex. He's old and he doesn't deserve to worry.'

'If he's that old, doesn't he deserve the freedom of his retirement?'

'He loves these roses. Don't you have something you love more than anything?'

There was a moment when a shadow crossed his face. 'I'm not welded to one place, one thing and certainly not one person.'

She only just refrained from rolling her eyes again. 'Well, lots of people are and what's more they actually *like* to be. Alex has handed over the rest of the grounds to your new garden maintenance company who come from stupidly far away, but the rose garden was his design, his planting, all his work. It's his treasure. He planted them for his late wife.'

'On someone else's property,' Rafael growled.

How could he be so uncaring?

He watched her through narrowed eyes. Then spoke again. 'If you don't come with me, you can go and tell your Alex that he's no longer needed to work here.'

Gracie gasped. 'Are you holding his job over me to make me go to your stupid party?'

He smiled, tightly.

'Wow. You must really be afraid of going by yourself if you're resorting to threats.'

Now he actually laughed. 'I'm not afraid to fight for what I want.'

'And you're not afraid to fight dirty.' She gritted her teeth in the face of his partial nudity. 'So you think the end justifies the means?'

'Not always. But often.'

'And you "often" bully your way into getting what you want?'

'Usually I buy what I want,' he replied carelessly. 'But I didn't want to offend you by offering you money.'

She flashed a filthy look at him. Of all the pompous things to say. 'Why not just ask nicely?'

He sighed deeply. 'Would you please go to the party with me? I'm new in town and I don't want to walk in alone.'

She didn't believe he was insecure for a second.

'You want me to go with you, dressed in my wet skirt and bruised knee?' She shook her head. 'I'm going into Bellezzo to watch the festival on the waterfront.'

'I can take care of your outfit,' he said softly.

'Excuse me?'

His grin was positively wicked and he leaned forward and scooped her into his arms again.

'This is assault,' she choked as she was pressed against all his hot naked skin. And muscles.

'What? This is gentlemanly behaviour. I've rescued a damsel in distress,' he countered as he marched through to a large living room. 'The least you can do in return is gift me a few hours of your precious time. Now…' He deposited her in a plush armchair and pointed to the corner. 'What do you think of these?'

Gracie gaped at the two racks of women's clothing. 'You have a ready supply of evening wear for occasions such as this?' She stared from the racks to him and back again. And then back at him because he was insanely fascinating. 'You enjoy dressing women?'

Something kindled in his eyes and she instantly knew his unspoken answer. He liked *undressing* them.

He walked towards the racks. 'They're using the villa for a fashion shoot tomorrow. These are the dresses they'll be modelling.'

A fashion shoot? *Models?* She turned to the hangers in horror. 'I won't fit into any of them.'

'I'm confident we can find something suitable.'

She glared at his tone—catching his gaze raking down her body.

'They'll be worth a lot of money,' she argued stiffly. 'I wouldn't want to damage one.' Except there were some gorgeous-looking fabrics on those hangers.

'If you want Alex to keep his job and keep his roses alive, then you'll get into one of these dresses and come along for the ride. It's only a party. I'm hardly proposing marriage.'

'If it's only a party, why can't you face it alone?' She straightened. 'Is someone you're afraid of seeing going to be there?' She warmed to the idea, intrigued by his playboy reputation. 'An ex?'

'Not tonight I don't think.' He adopted a faux thoughtful pose. 'Perhaps I need armour.'

'From all your stalkers?' She shook her head. 'You'd swat them away like flies.' No way was this man vulnerable.

He sighed again. 'I already told you the reason. I'm easily bored. I'd like a distraction.'

'You're easily bored? I pity you,' she mocked. 'People with good imaginations never get bored.'

'Oh, I have an imagination. Though right now it's probably best if I don't use it.'

She sent him a cool look.

'So what's your name?' He leaned back, smiling at her hesitation. 'I could call the police, you know. You are trespassing.'

Grimly she bit the bullet. 'My name is Grace James.'

'Grace.' He held out his hand. 'It's a pleasure to meet you.'

She couldn't be churlish enough to refuse his hand when he'd been carrying her about the place for the last twenty minutes, but she wasn't prepared for the electricity that shot through her the second her fingers clasped his. Quickly she pulled free, hiding her hand behind her back and clenching her fist to try to stop the lingering sizzling sensation. It didn't work. So she turned to the dresses and started sorting through the hangers.

'You're my fairy godmother,' she said with determined airiness. 'I might meet an amazing man there.'

'So you're single,' he said, while inspecting the second rack. 'Good to know.'

She gritted her teeth.

'I think this would suit you.' He pulled a gown from the rack and held it up to show her.

'It's white.' She glared at it. 'I'll have spilt something on it before we even get there.'

He laughed. 'It doesn't matter.'

'It matters.' With her luck it would be worse than a spill, she'd likely split the seam and she truly didn't want to make even more of a fool of herself tonight.

'You know you want to,' he said softly. 'Please.'

The man was an appalling flirt. As if he needed armour. There was no way this guy had any chinks. He had zero vulnerability. No, he was just a jaded playboy looking for light entertainment until his new batch of models turned up tomorrow. She wasn't going to give him anything.

But she *was* going to go to the Palazzo Chiara and experience something she never ordinarily would—glamour, exclusivity. Because she was living life on her own terms now. She wasn't missing out on anything.

'Fine,' she snapped, turning her back on the glittering smugness that instantly crossed his face. 'Where can I get changed?'

Ten minutes later, installed in the most ornate and massive bedroom she'd ever been in in her life, Gracie wriggled into the dress. It had taken her eight of those minutes to absorb the sumptuous decor of the elegant room. Now she glared at her reflection in the large free-standing mirror. No way could she wear a bra beneath it. Worse, she wasn't sure she could keep her knickers on either. The dress was so form-fitting her panty lines would be visible.

She blinked and wondered if she'd gone completely mad. What was she thinking by agreeing to this crazy idea? But, then, wouldn't she be equally mad to pass such a chance up? She'd never been able to accept any invitations as a child. She'd never gone to a classmate's house for a playdate, never walked into a swanky party as an actual *guest*… and she'd certainly never worn an eye-wateringly expensive designer dress like this before.

Breathing in deeply, she undid her bra and shimmied out of her undies, carefully putting them on the low armchair in the corner. This was one opportunity she was never going to get again, so she may as well go in braless and bold. Then she finger-combed her hair and twirled it into a low bun at the nape of her neck.

'Are you dressed yet? We need to get going or we'll miss the fireworks,' he called from outside the door.

With an overwhelming sense of mortification she stepped out from the room and refused to meet his eyes. 'I can't wear this. It's indecent.'

He was so silent she had to look up at him. He'd dressed in another tuxedo. How many did the guy have? Like the first, this fitted to perfection and was annoyingly gorgeous in the way it emphasised his lean, strong frame.

He regarded her for a full thirty seconds—so long she started to fidget with her watch strap.

'It's perfect,' he finally said. Roughly.

'It's far from perfect.' She looked down at the dress and put up her hand, self-consciously covering the neckline. 'It's pulling in all the wrong places.'

'Right places. Very right.'

'Because you like your dates to look—'

'Beautiful. Of course. I'm not sure the watch works, though.'

'Actually, it keeps good time and this Cinderella needs to keep an eye on it. I can't be out past midnight.'

'Because you might have too much fun?' He reached out and lifted her wrist. 'It's old.'

'It's vintage,' she corrected.

'It's a man's.'

'Yes,' she muttered defensively. It was very precious to her. 'An old man's watch.'

He released her startlingly quickly. 'Let's go. How is your knee?'

'Fine as long as I don't try to run. I'm keeping the sandals on.'

'Then I shall remain on hand as your long-suffering emergency support structure.'

'Thank you, I so appreciate that,' she cooed. 'If anyone asks me what I'm doing there, I'm going to tell them the truth,' she muttered.

'Marvellous.' He led her outside. 'I expect we'll have a ball.'

The car was low off the ground, red, polished to within an inch of its life and undoubtedly capable of screaming speed. She fastened her seatbelt.

'I won't be drinking, so I can drive home,' she said primly.

Her plan to abstain wasn't about driving but the insane attraction for him she was battling. If she had even a sniff of alcohol, she wasn't sure she could control the reckless temptation that seemed to have materialised inside her at the mere sight of him.

He sent her a look. 'Sure thing,' he said blandly. 'They'll have some very nice champagne there, though. You might like to try just one glass.'

'I'm not a risk-taker.' Definitely not around this man.

'Yet today you've trespassed on private property and are now going to a party in a borrowed designer dress with a man you barely know.'

'In a Ferrari, no less.' She nodded solemnly and

braced herself for his no doubt reckless driving skills. 'Most adventurous evening of my life so far.'

'That's…' He glanced at her, but his brows lifted and he didn't finish his comment. 'Why don't you take risks?'

Because she'd always had to hold back. Always been on the alert from years of conditioning, of watching over her shoulder and being cautious. But she had her safety plan figured out—she knew who Rafael was and Alex would call her in the morning if she didn't look in on him. And the imp in her wanted to have fun for once. It would be an experience.

'I struggle to open up and trust people.' She stared, amazed as Rafael began to laugh.

'Don't look like that!' She mock-punched his arm. 'I'm serious. What you're seeing is the *new* me. Opening up and delivering one hundred percent honesty. It's liberating.' She smiled.

'The new you,' he said, his smile not gone. 'One hundred percent honesty one hundred percent of the time?'

'Absolutely,' she said fervently.

He roared with laughter this time. '*No one* is that honest.'

'I am.'

'Definitely not you.'

'I *am*,' she said indignantly.

'Really? Could you be honest with someone even if you knew it was going to hurt them?' he asked. 'Isn't it better to play it safe sometimes and protect someone's feelings?'

That this guy thought about protecting someone's feelings surprised her. 'You'd actually protect another person's feelings?'

'Sure.'

So had he lied to her about how her dress looked? She just knew he had. 'I bet you send flowers and jewels when you leave your lovers.'

'That's not generally a good idea,' he said. 'I prefer to leave them breathless.'

'Oh, please.' She rolled her eyes.

'Well, you're absolutely the kind of person who cares about someone else's feelings, Ms I'll-Water-the-Roses-for-the-Old-Guy.'

'You say that like it's not a compliment.'

He laughed again.

'Not being honest hurts people more,' she said with soft passion. 'Because in the end the truth does always come out.'

He shook his head. 'You're so wrong. People lie and get away with it every day. Not just murderers. Cheats. Thieves. Everyday white lies as well.'

'But it eats them up *inside*,' she said softly. 'Sure, you may never know that someone has lied to you, but the *liar* knows. And the liar suffers for it. Even if they think they don't, they do. They're weakened. Each lie breaks them down piece by piece.'

His gaze intensified on her. 'Told a lot of lies in your lifetime?'

She held his gaze and her smile twisted. 'More than you'd ever believe.'

And she'd been weakened by every one.

CHAPTER THREE

'YOU'VE LIED YOUR head off your whole life?' Rafe didn't believe her. But he was drawn in by the shadows flickering in her eyes. 'Why so many lies?'

'For protection, as you suggested. But it still does damage and I refuse to lie any more.' She squared her shoulders and smiled. But it wasn't the bubbly smile he'd seen earlier when she'd been amongst the roses and he wondered if she was actually serious.

'I'm like you,' she said. 'Upfront about what I want out of my life. What I will accept, and what I won't.'

'What makes you think I'm upfront about what I want from my life?' How did she think she knew anything about him?

'You're decisive and take action to get what you want. The fact that I'm sitting in your car right now is a perfect example of your determination.'

Good point. He *was* used to getting his way, though honestly he'd not been certain she'd agree to attend the party with him. Even now he wouldn't be surprised if she slipped away once they arrived at the *palazzo*. He'd have to keep her occupied.

'But if this is the "new you", then you're getting what you want as well,' he teased.

He'd been absurdly satisfied when she'd said yes, but it had been his first victory of a less than stellar day and he'd take it.

'Once I'd had the time to process your...*invitation*, I realised it could be an interesting experience.' She nodded primly, but the effect was ruined when an effervescent smile lit up her face. 'Not one I'm likely to repeat.'

True, though why the fact should give him a twinge, he didn't know. He'd been feeling off all day. He'd deliberately not visited the Villa Rosetta until the refurbishment was complete, but while he could appreciate its beauty and value, there'd not been the pleasure of getting what he'd wanted for so long.

Fool. What had he expected? The decades-old promise that the villa represented had never been fulfilled and never *could* be. His father, Roland, was long since dead. And that finality left an unusual melancholy just beneath his skin.

So not Rafe. He never wasted time looking backwards, he pushed forward, making headway against the resistance he was accustomed to. He pushed harder than anyone because he'd always had to. Illegitimate, unwanted heir that he was. Securing the villa should have been a pinnacle moment but it was larger than he'd realised. Its vastness screamed out for more people to be living in it. For the family he'd never had.

Fool. He wasn't eight years old and full of fairy-tale dreams for a loving family now.

The woman wandering about the grounds had been a welcome distraction. He'd watched from the villa, initially outraged at her blithe trespassing. But he'd grown increasingly intrigued as she'd strolled through the roses with that smile lighting up her face.

'The fireworks are supposed to be spectacular,' she said as she waited for him to start the car. 'You're promising me all the fireworks, right?'

He glanced at her profile—had she really meant that as innocently as it had sounded? She turned to look at him fully, her expression limpid. The longer he looked at her, the deeper the colour ran in her cheeks. He was fascinated by the hint of vulnerability in her reaction.

'What?' she suddenly snapped. 'Do I have something on my nose?'

He shook his head slowly. 'Are you flirting with me?'

'What? No!' That colour in her cheeks ran crimson now. 'Hurry up and drive. I want to see the fireworks. I've been looking forward to them all day.'

Warmth flowed through his veins. 'I wouldn't mind if you were flirting with me.'

Her mouth opened, then closed, then her eyes narrowed. 'You're shocking, you know that?' She stared straight ahead as if to ignore him. But then suddenly turned to snap at him again. 'Does everyone flirt with you?'

'Mostly.' Still grinning, he finally started the engine, enjoying the crazy whim that had led him to take a total stranger to the most exclusive party on the European continent.

Her eyes had hit him the second he'd been able to see again after wiping all that water from his own. Large and framed with long lashes, they were caramel-coloured and captivated him completely. When he added her flawless, lightly tanned skin, providing a perfect backdrop for those wide eyes and lovely curving lips, it made for pretty. Her long hair was tied back in a bun but had hints of blonde and brown in the loose tendrils that curled about her sweetheart-shaped face...

Yes, it all added up to his new definition of gorgeous. She was on the shorter side, with curves in the places he appreciated most. That worn denim skirt had stopped just at her knees and shown smooth-looking legs, while her blouse had been floral. He'd liked the way the buttons had strained to contain her breasts. He'd imagined popping them open one by one. But in the end it had been the melted caramel colour of her eyes—all sweet warmth—that he'd kept returning to. There was a lightness in them that he found unusual, enchanting, *sweet*.

Rafe did not do *sweet*. Rafe did sophisticated. It was safer to play with women who knew the rules of the one-night-only game. But fresh, half-wet, funny Grace intrigued him. Temptation had been irresistible and reckless.

So now here she was alongside him, wearing a killer dress that emphasised every one of those bountiful curves. He wanted to kiss down that deep scooped neckline and feel her lean closer for more. His muscles tensed.

Well, he *had* been celibate for six weeks—virtually a marathon for him and the longest stretch in his adult life. He gritted his teeth and concentrated on the winding road. Grace was *not* a one-night-stand prospect. She wasn't the type. When she'd said this was the most adventurous night of her life so far, she'd meant it.

A small army of models was arriving at the villa tomorrow. There'd be more than one to frolic with afterwards if he still wanted to. Frankly, though, the speculation didn't excite him.

He glanced at Grace again and wished he had that hose once more. If that dress were wet, it'd turn translucent and he'd know for certain that she wore nothing beneath it. He suspected so, he could almost see the outline of her nipples. He shifted in his seat and touched his foot harder on the accelerator, irritated with his sudden descent into basic thinking. Was he suddenly some hormonal teen? The sooner they got to the party, the sooner he could get a grip on himself.

Palazzo Chiara was lit up like a fairy-tale castle. He pulled up by the waiting valet and scooted around to help Grace out before she tripped on the stones or something equally unfortunate. But his half-sarcastic gallantry was rewarded when he saw the look on her face as she gazed at the *palazzo*.

'You like it?' He couldn't help smiling at her reaction.

'It's *huge*.'

'The Villa Rosetta is big.' He puffed out his chest.

Her eyes kindled with amusement. 'You're defensive about size? I never would have suspected you'd be so insecure.'

'I told you I needed armour tonight.' He winked. 'You think it's better than the Villa Rosetta?'

'Nothing is better than Alex's roses,' she declared loyally. 'This place is *too* huge. It's beautiful, but it's not a home. The Villa Rosetta is a home—you can sense the love in it.'

Her genuine words touched a raw spot and he refrained from replying by guiding her into the reception hall. A liveried waiter stepped forward with a gleaming silver tray laden with tall champagne flutes.

'You're sure you don't want a drink?' Rafe teased her.

She shook her head. He passed on the offer as well and walked her further into the room so she could appreciate the gold and marble interior. Her breathy gasps delighted him and he kept walking, aware of heads turning. He carefully avoided eye contact with a couple of the models due at the villa tomorrow. He didn't want to be interrupted yet. Grace's face was fascinatingly mobile and it was impossible for her to hide her reactions. Captivated, he pointed out more of the various features—from the tumbling crystal chandeliers to the sparkling waterfall in the centre of the room. But she saw some of the people looking their way and definitely recognised some.

'Famous people,' she noted quietly. 'Rich people.'

'Rich *and* famous people.' He nodded.

'A Venn diagram of the upper echelon.' She nodded. 'And just one outside the circle.'

'Is that one feeling self-conscious?'

'Absolutely. But she's absolutely determined to get over herself.'

He laughed, liking her frankness.

'Pleasure to see you here, Rafe.' Toby Winters, a party-hard aristocratic banker with a vast holiday estate on the lake, interrupted them loudly. 'I heard work on Villa Rosetta is complete. Welcome to the neighbourhood.'

'Thank you,' he said calmly. 'Julia, lovely to see you.'

Julia, Toby's wife, was too busy looking Grace over to bother answering. Besides, Toby had intervened again.

'You're racking up quite the portfolio,' Toby said. 'I envy your energy.'

Rafe smiled but tuned into the conversation that was occurring about a foot lower than his eye level, where Julia was interrogating his fish-out-of-water guest.

'I'm only here because he made me come,' Grace said.

Oh, Lord. Did she have any idea how that husky comment was going to be interpreted?

Grace had offered Julia a disarming smile, but Julia wouldn't disarm in any way.

'He made you?' Julia's eyebrows might have risen had her forehead not been fixed in place by the poison she'd injected beneath her skin.

'I'm working for him.' Grace blushed. 'C-currently... Just for...' She trailed off.

Rafe gritted his teeth to stay serious.

'You work for Rafe?' Julia asked archly.

Grace, in her oblivious innocence, nodded.

'Yes.' Julia raked Grace over from head to toe with a frigid glare. 'I can see exactly in what capacity you work for him.'

Because Grace didn't look like a PA or a secretary or a housekeeper or even a gardener. Julia grabbed her husband's arm and all but dragged him away. Grace turned shocked eyes on Rafe, her pretty skin now stained scarlet.

'She thinks I'm…'

She couldn't bring herself to say it. And she was blushing again. Rafe threw his head back and laughed. She was stunned at Julia's interpretation. That meant she was even more naive and innocent than he'd already suspected. In her skirt and floral shirt she'd looked sweetly gorgeous. In the killer white dress she looked both voluptuous and shy and it made for a mouth-watering combination. But he wanted to ease her embarrassment now. So he opted to tease.

'A paid escort?' He nodded. 'I believe so. You were the one who answered the question.'

'It's this dress.' She put her hand up to hide that glorious cleavage. 'I told you it was indecent.' She paused as a thought struck her and she blinked rapidly. 'Why would they think *you* would require the services of a paid escort?'

The compliment hidden in there was so unguarded it made it all the more touching. Something was seriously wrong with him. He could not be going crazy with lust for some random woman he'd found wandering in his garden…

'Why wouldn't I?' he answered idly. 'You weren't exactly keen on being my date. I had to pressure you to come.'

And, yes, he'd meant her to catch that lame double entendre that Julia had already picked up on. He'd like nothing more than to make Grace come.

She flushed even more beautifully. 'Because I don't know you. Anyway, you didn't ask me because you wanted to date me. You wanted to pay me back for ruining your suit.'

'Did I?'

She stared up at him, her eyes melting. 'Stop it. You're an appalling flirt. It's like you can't help yourself.'

Right now it seemed he couldn't. 'Who says I'm flirting?'

Rafe watched Grace roll her eyes with outlandish expressiveness and then she glanced past him. 'I'm hungry. Isn't there any food?'

'People are here to be seen, not to scoff.'

'Heaven forbid they be seen munching.' She looked about some more before a small pout of disappointment drew his attention to her lips. 'I think I'll have a drink after all.'

He signalled a passing waiter and lifted a flute of champagne off the tray for her. 'Are you sure?'

'One won't hurt me.'

More people came over—offering congratulations and conversation, soliciting his attention and seeking to satisfy their own curiosity. Grace was oddly quiet as he chatted, offering only a nod as he introduced her to them as his friend. He watched her out of the corner of his eye, noting how swiftly the champagne was disappearing from her glass. She was sipping to stop herself from speaking, he just knew it. And the sparkle in her eyes was growing brighter by the second. Turning abruptly, he excused them both from the company and walked her towards the open doorway for some fresh air.

'They all want something from you.' Grace drained the last drop from the crystal flute. 'Honestly, they were all over you like some hideous disease. Every last one, sucking up.'

He was the one wanting to suck up. He couldn't take his eyes from her mouth and he really needed to get a grip. 'Everybody wants something from me. Attention. Money,' he said dryly. Everything always came back to money. And he was under no illusion that if he had none, those people wouldn't come within fifty feet of him.

'I don't want either of those things,' she said cheerfully.

No, it seemed she might not. But maybe he could make her change her mind on the attention front.

'Let's go look at the lake. It must be fireworks time soon.' She walked out the wide-flung doors but came to an abrupt halt on the patio. 'Who's that guy?' she whispered loudly, nodding her head in the direction of a tall, grey-haired man icily glaring at Rafe from further along the marble patio.

Rafe met the man's stare for a second, then deliberately turned away. 'No one important.'

Maurice Butler would never again have any importance in his life.

'Yeah, right.' She smothered a laugh. 'If looks could kill, you'd both be dead.'

'He's a business acquaintance,' he lied.

'Really?' She shot him a look. 'I don't believe you.'

'Look at the lanterns.' He pointed in the opposite direction.

He wanted to be alone with Grace, all his attention on her and her attention only on him.

'But he's coming over. He looks like he wants to talk to you.'

'Well, I don't wish to talk to him.' Rafe firmly took her hand and walked her down to the lakefront.

'It's beautiful.'

The lights were reflected in her eyes and flickered across her face. She was so pretty. Sinful whispers swirled in his head, all the things he'd do to her, with her, for her. All the things he probably shouldn't.

'You're using me to avoid talking to anyone else,' she noted as they walked to the water's edge.

'Yes. It's working well.'

'Why did you bother coming at all if you didn't want to talk to them?'

'To be seen.'

'Because?'

'Because I'm here and they can't ignore that fact.'

'You have history with these people? With that man?'

He hesitated for a moment, but what did it matter if she knew? 'That man you just asked about is my nephew. I heard he wanted to buy the villa. Unfortunately for him, *I* was the successful bidder.'

'Your *nephew*?' She turned around to stare again at the man still standing on the patio just outside the wide-open doors. He knew she was processing the vast age difference. Maurice was thirty-two years older than he.

'You wanted to beat him more than you actually wanted the home?' she asked, her eyes narrowing.

'No, I wanted the villa.' He turned to look out at the water so he didn't have to see anyone from the family who'd made his life hell. 'I always wanted the villa.'

He didn't know why he'd admitted that to her— he presented it to everyone as the requisite luxury Italian holiday home string to his property portfolio.

'Why?' she asked.

'Childhood dream,' he muttered dryly. Thing was, it was true. He'd wanted it all his life. But it seemed the joke was on him. Walking into that villa this afternoon, he'd only felt emptier than ever.

'But you also enjoyed stealing it from under your nephew's nose,' she added shrewdly.

Rafe smiled bitterly. He had, of course. Blocking Maurice's interest in the villa had been a bonus point in the transaction.

'You're clearly not close.'

'Clearly not.' He straightened, determined to dismiss this conversation.

The fact that the villa had come with a pretty nymph in the garden was the one highlight of the day. He wasn't squandering the possibilities by getting bogged down in the past now. 'I didn't bring you along to have you pry into my personal life,' he said lazily, slipping back into Lothario mode. 'Entertain me another way.'

Her eyes widened. 'You're one arrogant ass, you know that?'

He did, actually. But he wasn't used to his dates calling him on it—at least, not quite so soon in his acquaintance. And never with amusement—it was with anger that they'd hurl that insult at him. Frankly, right now he *was* using his vast experience of arrogance to keep her burgeoning curiosity at bay. He hadn't brought her along to *talk* to him about those things but to look at and to laugh with and, yes, possibly explore the sensual promise he'd felt flare between them from the second they'd met. But he liked that she called him on it.

Struggling with conflicting emotions, he took

a hurried couple of paces to catch up to her. 'I'm sorry.' He caught her hand in his and fell into step. 'That was rude. I was uncomfortable talking about him. I don't want to talk about him.'

'That's totally fair enough. But you could have just said that and I'd have respected it.'

'Would you?' he asked pointedly.

She looked at him for a moment and then grinned sheepishly. 'I am hopelessly curious about people, so probably not.'

He grinned back, refreshed again by her candour. 'You're this curious about everyone?'

'Oh, yes.' She nodded emphatically. 'People fascinate me.'

That response was stupidly flattering, because he knew it was the truth. That was why she knew the gardener's life story, why she knew the history of the village. Grace James was one of those rare people who was genuinely *nice*. Interested in other people, in their stories and their lives. But why be so interested—what was lacking in her own life?

'People find you fascinating too,' he said.

She laughed at that. 'No. No, they don't. And don't feel you have to flatter me by arguing the point. Oh, look!'

He followed the direction of her deliberate distraction. Sure enough, she was watching other people again. He frowned at the scene going on at the edge of the *palazzo*'s private beach. A proposal no less. The fool was on bended knee, there was a trio of musicians and inevitably there was a guy with a camera filming the whole thing. Thankfully it only took a few moments.

Rafe watched Grace as she watched the happy couple kiss.

'Public proposals are so vain,' he muttered.

'*You're* calling them out for being vain?' She laughed mischievously and sent him a look from beneath her thick lashes. 'I think it's romantic. With all those lights on the water, and the warm breeze and the full moon and the music…it's perfect. They'll never forget it.'

'Of course they won't, because it's all been filmed for posterity. No doubt an edited clip will be uploaded onto the Internet before the night is over.' He shook his head. 'Such moments should be private. Not for show.'

'Why, Rafael.' She turned to face him, her eyes and skin illuminated by the soft warm glow of a hundred floating lanterns. 'You're a romantic.'

'I'm *what*?' he asked, startled.

'A romantic,' she marvelled triumphantly.

'No.' He tapped her on the nose with his finger. 'I meant making a mistake like that should definitely be kept private.'

'A mistake?'

'Marriage,' he growled.

'Of course you're against marriage. It would narrow the field too much for you.'

'That's right,' he agreed wickedly. 'Life's too short to settle down and be with just one person for ever. How boring.'

'Oh, that's right, you're easily bored. You're a billionaire with a feeble imagination.'

'Trust me, my imagination is all good.'

She shook her head and turned back to the couple. 'Well, I don't think it's boring at all.'

'*You're* the romantic,' he said. Of course she was. 'You know it never works out,' he said softly.

She looked back at him with amused speculation in her eyes. 'Are you talking of your own relationships?'

'Anyone's. Everyone's.'

'So, let me guess…' She studied him impishly. 'You're never getting married. Never having children.'

'Absolutely not.' He half laughed.

'Because your parents weren't happily married?'

'My parents weren't married at all,' he said simply.

'And you think that's scandalous in today's world?' She grinned. 'What do you think having unmarried parents means?'

'That I'm a bastard.' He winked at her. 'You have officially been warned.'

'You do know that lots of kids are born out of wedlock and lots of people divorce.'

He wasn't an idiot. He knew the stats. But his family situation had some extra spice that hadn't stilled the gossips' tongues. 'My father was over seventy when I was born. I have nephews almost twice my age. My half-siblings were not impressed when my mother and I came along.' And he shouldn't be talking about this.

'They made life tough for you both?'

Tougher than this pretty nymph could ever imagine. It wasn't just the age gap between his parents but the education, background, social status… *everything and everyone* had made life tough. Especially for his mother. What they'd done to her he'd never forget, or forgive.

'Did your parents love each other?' she asked softly.

And there it was, that romantic nature of hers. The truth would crush all her idealistic dreams. 'You think that love could possibly make a difference?' He forced a laugh.

'So handsome yet so cynical.' She sighed. 'Such a shame.'

He leaned closer, playing up so he could forget the past. 'Handsome is a win, though, right?'

'A very small one,' she said, flattening him again.

But he'd seen the gleam in her eyes.

'Not that small.' He couldn't resist any more and put his hands on her waist. 'You're going to deny we have chemistry?'

'It's probably because we're polar opposites.'

That she didn't deny it surprised him all over again. He'd been expecting playful outrage and a pout. Instead, he just got a steadying hand on his chest and an assessing look.

'You're crazy good looking,' she said, her gaze narrowing on him. 'Like, not-of-this-earth good looking. And confident. So I'm guessing you know what you're doing when it comes to women. And I know I'm nothing like the women you usually bring along to these things. Given how much you like women, you probably would try anything once. For the novelty factor.'

'Are you suggesting I'm not discerning?' He couldn't decide whether to be pleased by her compliment about his looks or insulted by her assumption that he lacked pickiness when it came to women. But then he realised it wasn't only him she was insulting. 'And don't denigrate yourself.'

She looked up at him, that impish light flickering in her eyes. 'Oh, I'm not. But let's be honest, I'm not your type. Everyone here knows it. That's why they're staring.'

He didn't like the thought that he was predictable enough to have a 'type', even though he knew he did. 'That's not why they're staring.'

They were staring because she was a breath of fresh air—basically barefoot in those flimsy sandals, with her white dress gleaming in the light and her skin glowing in the radiance of all those lanterns. She was stunning. He—like the rest of them—couldn't take his eyes off her.

She, however, didn't appear to suffer the same problem when it came to him.

'There's a boat coming.' She craned her neck to peer past his shoulder. 'Everyone is walking over. Do you know who's on board?'

He didn't know, didn't care. Just wanted her eyes on him again.

'This party is non-stop drama,' she said. 'Are your "elite" events always like this?'

'Don't you go to parties very often?'

'Usually I'm serving the food.'

She was a waitress? That fitted with the travelling. She certainly wasn't a local with that softened English accent. Yet it surprised him. She had an unworldliness about her, as if her optimism and hopefulness hadn't yet been crushed by the harsh realities of life. Most travellers he'd met had a few street smarts and sharper edges. Maybe she was new to it all. His body tightened inappropriately again.

'What are we going to do about it?' he muttered harshly, unable to hold back his runaway thoughts.

'About what?'

Astounded, he turned her back to face him. 'This chemistry.'

'Nothing.' She turned back to watch the launch arrive. 'Do you think it's someone famous?'

He didn't give a damn if it was the Queen of England. He just wanted her attention back on him. 'I don't think this is something we can do nothing about.'

'Of course we can.' She laughed, but she didn't meet his eyes.

'You're not in the least curious?'

She finally focused on him properly. 'I'm sure you could make me feel amazing.' That giveaway colour washed over her light golden tan again. 'I'm sure you could make me want anything and everything. But I'm also positive you'd be bad news.'

'Bad news?' How could anything so explosive be bad news? 'Do you take everything so seriously?'

'Do you take everything so flippantly?'

'Not everything. No. But life is for living.' He tugged her closer. 'You should live a little.'

She smiled at that. 'That was a lame attempt at persuasion. I think you can do better.'

'Lame?' Was she critiquing his flirting skills? What had she said, that he was 'appalling'?

'You should stop trying to tempt me,' she said with disarming solemnity.

'Okay,' he lied. It wasn't okay.

That guileless look in her eyes was undermined by the knowing curve of her smile. 'I don't want to play games, Mr Vitale.'

He'd never met a woman who didn't want to play games. 'You calling me Mr Vitale *is* playing games.'

She drew a sharp breath. 'Okay. Honestly? I don't want to get hurt.'

'I don't hurt women.'

She sent him another look.

'I don't ever *want* to hurt women,' he clarified. 'I would never want to hurt you.'

He felt her shiver as he took her hand.

'You're cramping my style,' she said a little breathlessly. 'Step away, the nice guys aren't going to approach when you're circling me like a shark.'

'There aren't any nice guys here.'

Her nose wrinkled. 'Not any?'

'None. They're all sharks. They all want the same thing I do.'

'And what's that?'

The lanterns cast a light glow on her fine features. She looked luminous and delicate and she'd melt against him in a delicious bundle of soft heat. One kiss wouldn't end the world, would it?

She suddenly stepped backwards. 'That would be a mistake.'

She turned to watch the crowds greet whoever had arrived on that launch.

She was *very* focused on watching what other people were doing. On not looking at him. Was that her way of trying to keep this chemistry sealed? Didn't she realise that trying to bottle it would only cause a bigger explosion once the pressure grew too great? Smiling, he gently shook her.

'What?' She finally looked at him.

'Most women don't spend a date with me looking out for other men.'

'Am I not paying you enough attention?' She widened her eyes. 'I'm so sorry.'

'No, you're not,' he growled. That apology had been the most insincere thing to fall from her lips tonight. 'You're deliberately avoiding looking at me. I wonder why.'

'You have to wonder?' she scoffed. 'This isn't a *date*. This is coercion.'

'You don't know what coercion is.' He laughed. 'I didn't have to bully you so very much.'

She buttoned her lips and a small frown pleated that space between her eyebrows. 'I wanted to see the fireworks.'

He laughed again.

'It's the truth.'

'I'm sure it is.' He framed her face in his hands so he could look into her eyes the way he'd wanted to from the moment he'd first seen her.

'What are you doing?' she asked in the gentlest whisper.

'Getting closer.'

'Why?'

'Fireworks.' He leaned close enough to feel her sweet breath on his face. 'This still isn't coercion, by the way. This is seduction.'

'Is it?' She shook her head ever so slightly. 'You're very...tall,' she muttered weakly. 'And strong. You picked me up—'

'Easily, and the caveman in me enjoyed that. But I promise I won't do anything you don't want me to. What do you think?'

'I think you're a silver-tongued devil with decades of experience at making women feel good.'

'Decades? How old do you think I am?'

'In terms of experience you're ancient, whereas I'm a mere babe in the woods.'

'Are you? Why's that?' He watched her pupils dilate, filling with her secrets.

She didn't answer.

'Caramellina,' he murmured again, lost in the warm depths of her gaze and the soft feel of her skin beneath his fingers. 'You even smell sweet.' An intoxicating combination of roses and vanilla.

He stared into her luminous eyes for a long time and for every moment of it she met his gaze. They stood, stilled in that silent connection until he saw it—that sensual curiosity that he felt, revealed and reflected in her. More than curiosity, it was a pull that could no longer be ignored. Her lips parted and the smallest of sighs escaped her.

'Oh, all right, then, do your worst,' she breathed.

He chuckled. 'I think you mean my best.'

'Whatever, just get it over with.'

Her breathing was a little quick and he paused. 'I wouldn't want to bother someone unwilling.' He softened his hold on her.

'I'm not unwilling.' She almost ground her teeth.

He half laughed again. 'No?'

'No,' she snapped. 'Just kiss me already.'

He brushed his lips over hers as gently as he was able to, desperately trying to go slowly because she was flighty. He'd pull out every trick he knew to tempt her closer, so she wouldn't startle and step back. He wanted this too much.

She felt like a fragile flower and he didn't want to crush her. But then her soft lips parted and she let him in. With his first real taste the attempt to go slowly became strained. Then he felt her tongue shyly seeking, and her arms slid up his back.

His chest tightened and he abandoned all idea of going slowly. Any kind of strategy burned as pure instinct blew his brain out. The kiss was hungry and hot and hard in the thud of a heartbeat. To his immense pleasure, she rose more to meet him, her soft curves pressing against him as a sultry moan escaped her. It felt like the first drink after a long thirst, like finding an oasis after months in the desert. She was lush and sweet and so responsive he lost his head completely.

He swept his hands over her body, feeling for himself that, yes, there was no bra beneath that tight, white sheath, neither was there any underwear at all. Desire stabbed so hard he hauled her closer still, deepening the kiss to a completely carnal one. He wanted more of it—more of the softness in her embrace, more of her ardent response, more of her sweet, sultry heat. He wanted everything.

He was so taken aback by the way she melted that all he could do was pull her closer until they were sealed from lips to hips in a passionate, never-ending force of hunger. Finesse and skill and seduction be damned. This was too elemental for that. She was too elemental—with unexpected depths and desire.

At the sound of thunderclaps overhead they broke apart. Breathing hard, he glanced up at the explosion of colour raining across the sky.

Damn fireworks.

Grace released a long breath and then he heard her delighted gust of laughter.

'It's so beautiful.'

He kept hold of her hands. He wanted her back in his arms, but her hands would have to do because he refused to curtail her enjoyment of this. He watched the colours above reflected in her eyes and skin and waited for the sky to go silent again. Finally, blessedly, it did.

'Show's over,' he said, his voice husky.

'I guess it's time to go home,' she agreed quietly.

As he led her to his car he kept hold of her hand, rubbing his thumb over hers. He didn't want this warmth to literally slip through his fingers. In that bleak emptiness this afternoon he'd never have imagined his evening would end with such a sweet, insatiable lover in his bed.

'That was spectacular.' She sighed contentedly and snuggled lower in the passenger seat.

He quite agreed.

'I really liked the massive one at the end. It was like a kaleidoscope of colours.'

His hands tightened on the wheel. Was she talking about the actual fireworks? Not the kiss they'd shared? He half choked at being levelled with a casual comment. He'd have to straighten out her priorities. He had far better fireworks than those on the agenda for her.

She quietened as he cruised along the winding lakefront road towards Bellezzo and the Villa Rosetta beyond. The warm breeze tempered the thudding desire roaring through his system. He had no desire to race. Anticipation feathered across his skin like hot silk. He'd take his time and treat her to absolute, exquisite torture. For the first time in weeks he felt invigorated.

'You're coming back to the villa with me, aren't you, Grace?' he asked softly. But he got no response.

He glanced at her and then braked in surprise. 'Grace? Grace?'

In the moonlight she was unbearably beautiful. And she simply had to come back with him now given he had no idea where in the village she was staying.

'Grace?'

It seemed he wasn't about to get a sensible answer out of her either. Because the maddening, unpredictable minx had fallen fast asleep.

CHAPTER FOUR

GRACIE DREW THE soft blanket closer and blinked sleepily at the beam of light streaming through the small gap in the curtains. She didn't want it to be morning. She didn't want to go to work. She didn't...*know where the heck she was*!

She jerked upright, staring in amazement at the beautiful furnishings. She was in that massive bedroom in the Villa Rosetta. Mortifying memories slammed into her mind, eviscerating the last of her blissful sleep fog—the crazy hose, that designer dress, that exquisite *kiss*.

Her pulse fired like a sprinter false-starting from the blocks.

Okay, she was better off not remembering the kiss. Her skin burned and she threw back the blanket covering her. She huffed a relieved sigh when she saw she was still wearing the white dress.

She frowned. The last thing she could recall was getting into Rafael's car to leave the party. How could she not remember anything more? She'd had only the one glass of champagne. Wild imagination took flight—had her drink been spiked?

She mentally put herself through a physical. She had no abnormal aches or tenderness anywhere. No horrible headache or yucky taste in her mouth. No certain intuition or fear… Only embarrassment.

Yes. The embarrassing truth was she'd been working insanely long hours and yesterday she'd had too little food and just enough champagne to cause a temporary case of narcolepsy. *Mortifying.*

She glanced across the large room and saw her blouse, skirt and underwear on the plush chair where she'd left them last night, only now her phone was with them. Rafael must've put it there for her. So he definitely knew she hadn't been wearing underwear with this dress.

The cool air from the ceiling fan did nothing to stop the last of her pride smouldering into cinders. He'd put her to bed because she'd fallen asleep on the drive home and apparently he hadn't been able to wake her. She'd probably been snoring. Or drooling. Or both. She slumped back on the bed, hauling the blanket up like a shroud, willing immediate death.

Her heart denied her, not only refusing to stop but actually sprinting faster, while her equally fickle mind circled back to the highlight of the night.

Not the fireworks. That *kiss.*

She closed her eyes, toes curling as the merest whisper of memory sent sensations cascading through her. She sighed and resolutely opened her eyes again. This reaction was over the top. It wasn't like she'd never kissed a guy before. In fact, she'd kissed four—though they'd all turned out to be frogs, no fairy-tale charming princes. It had been a bit like kissing frogs too—cold and slimy—and she'd not been tempted to go further with any of them.

But with Rafael? He was *definitely* no fairy-tale for ever prince, but what did that matter when with that one kiss he'd obliterated all her preconceived ideas of intimacy? Everything she'd thought—that she needed to be in love, that she needed to truly know and trust a guy before she'd be able to experience real pleasure in intimacy—*wasn't true*. It turned out she didn't need all that. She just needed a man of experience, talent and arrogance. She just needed Rafael. And she was so much shallower than she'd believed herself to be. Fallen angel good looks were all it took.

She might be mortified by her exhaustion, but she'd been saved by it too. Because it would've taken only another ten minutes in his company and she'd have tossed caution to the wind and let him do anything he wanted—she'd have cheered him on, in fact.

What had happened to her rational, sane, completely careful self?

Her hidden impulsive side reared again—hitting out at the control she'd just sought to retrieve again. She'd *wanted* that wildness. She could kick herself for falling asleep so quickly and deeply, like some overtired toddler. She'd *wanted* what she'd instinctively known he could give her. That was why she'd gone with him in the first place. But that kind of recklessness wasn't truly her, was it?

She flung the beautiful blanket off once more and this time snapped right out of bed. *Fool.* She'd had the opportunity for one amazing night, for one blistering moment, and she'd muffed it. He must think her so *weird*, like Sleeping-freaking-Beauty in reverse, falling into a deep sleep *after* the kiss of her life. But maybe he hadn't tried that hard to wake her. Which meant he hadn't wanted more kissing…

Even more mortifying.

She wriggled out of the beautiful dress and hung it over the back of another plush armchair. In two minutes she was back in her own clothes and tip-toeing through the vast villa, offering thanks that her knee was only slightly stiff. She had to escape without facing Rafael Vitale again. It was early enough for her to get to work on time and no one would know she'd stayed here. Not that she'd be embarrassed, but…well, she'd be a bit embarrassed.

She made it outside, but she had to take a second to appreciate the truly cinematic view. Dawn bathed the lake and garden in that golden magic. She couldn't resist darting across the lawn to breathe in the beauty of Alex's roses one last time. The gentle warmth of that just rising sun released their light, sweet scent. Impulsively she decided to take Alex not just a photo, but an actual flower—a perfect example of his amazing work would make his morning. She reached out to pick one of the distinctive creamy-coloured roses, but the plant wasn't keen to relinquish one of its prize blossoms. She tugged harder to snap the stem.

'What are you doing?'

The question sounded right in her ear. With a yelp she spun around, releasing the rose but scratching the fleshy part below her thumb on a thorn as she did so.

'Ow.' She shook out her hand and glared at Rafael. '*Why* must you sneak up on people?'

Why must he always look so impossibly handsome? Why was he even *dressed*? He was all in black—jeans, T—and his hair was a touch damp as if he'd had the time to shower already. But it was super early—shouldn't he still be in bed? She froze as her reckless imagination instantly conjured up accompanying images to that tantalising thought. A wave of extreme heat scorched her cheeks and her chest and other places too personal to mention.

The freeze gave way to the fidgets as she practically paced on the spot, seeking a way to get past him. But he was planted on the narrow grass path like an immovable plinth of pure masculinity.

'Why must you sneak around my garden?' he countered easily, his eyebrows lifting as he watched her wriggle like a damn fish on a line in front of him. 'What are you doing?'

'What does it look like I'm doing?'

'Stealing.' He grabbed her hand, lifting it to inspect the damage she'd just so uselessly done to herself.

A thin line of blood was rapidly filling the annoyingly deep scratch. Though once more she didn't feel a damn thing. It was official, Rafael Vitale was the embodiment of the best anaesthetic ever.

But he was frowning. 'We need to get a plaster on that.'

She tugged her hand from his, as electricity sent her pulse to attack point. 'It's not fatal.'

'I wouldn't want to take any chances on that.'

She braved a glance back up at him. That handsome smile? The warmth in those bewitchingly dark brown eyes? The man was back to flirt mode and it was too unfair of him to sneak up on her when he was looking so fine. He hadn't shaved and his morning stubble made him look more like trouble than ever. Devastating, delicious, sinful trouble. She bit her lip, holding back all the apologies. *No nervous babbling now.*

'Come back inside,' he invited, confirming his position as the greatest temptation of her life. 'We'll cover that cut and have breakfast.'

'That's very kind, but no, thank you,' she replied, trying to hold on to some sanity.

Naturally, however, her stomach chose that exact moment to rumble with volume and vigour. She stared into his eyes as her stomach growled on. No way could he not hear the thunder of her disloyal digestive system. Would *nothing* go right? Could she not even manage a simple escape from him and be left with even a snippet of dignity?

'I thought you were always honest?' he teased softly.

She cleared her throat awkwardly. 'I didn't say I'm not hungry. I just can't stay for breakfast. I need to get going.'

'You're trying to get away from me?'

'It's not just you,' she corrected dryly. 'I have to get to work.'

His smile was a devastating combination of smug and boyishly cute. 'But I make you uncomfortable.'

'I'm embarrassed,' she corrected. 'I fell asleep in your car. For all I know, I was drooling when you carried me into your house—again. And I'm not a featherweight. It's a wonder you didn't put your back out.'

'There was no drooling. No snoring. And I liked carrying you. You were very sweet and snuggly.'

That blush burned every inch of her skin again.

'Very difficult to walk away from,' he added softly.

Her breath stalled in her lungs. She didn't want to think about him putting her on that massive bed—he'd have held her so closely, he'd have been bent over her...

'And now here you are, stealing roses, like Beauty.'

'Does that make you the Beast?' she asked, pulling her brain back from those unhelpful visions and trying to put some distance between them.

He inclined his head and his gaze lowered, focusing on a spot just behind her. 'I don't think your Alex will be pleased to see you've mangled his prize rose bush.'

She turned, guiltily regarding the way that rose was now dangling half-torn from the branch. 'I thought it would snap off easily.'

'They're for *looking* at,' he said. 'Not destroying.'

'I wanted to take one to Alex,' she confessed, sending him an apologetic look, 'so he'd see how well they were doing and would stop worrying.'

Rafael glanced at her again, his expression veiled. In the ensuing moment of silence he slowly reached and took her hand again. Gracie hoped he hadn't felt her tiny shiver at the moment of connection.

He said nothing, just dropped his gaze to study

the trail of red snaking across her skin. 'I really think you need a plaster.'

She couldn't be ungracious again, not when that trickle of blood had turned into a bit of a stream and she didn't want to come across as petty or rude. He didn't deserve that. 'I'm sorry to put you to so much trouble.'

'Are you?' His lashes swiftly lifted, amusement flashing in his eyes. 'Yet you think I'm a beast?'

She eyed him suspiciously at the mournfulness in his tone. 'Are you fishing for compliments?'

'I always need compliments this early in the morning.'

'You're not so bad, I suppose,' she said slowly, but realised, as she said it, that it was true. She huffed out a breath and tried again. 'Well, actually, you're really honourable.' She couldn't meet his gaze as she walked back to the villa, focusing intently on not slipping over again. The guy had women falling at his feet, she literally couldn't do that again. 'I was in a vulnerable position last night and I appreciate you taking care of me. Thank you.'

He didn't immediately reply and she snuck a look at him. A smile had transformed his face from handsome to heart-stopping and she had to look away again.

'It was my pleasure,' he eventually replied. 'You know, I've never had a woman fall asleep…' he paused meaningfully as he opened the door and waited for her to walk inside ahead of him '…in my Ferrari before.'

Oh, he was being Mr Provocative again?

'You mean in your scintillating company?' She rolled her eyes. 'You really are a conceited creature.'

'I did wonder if you'd hit your head, not your knee.' He laughed, unabashed, and led her through to that glorious kitchen again.

'So you thought I must have been concussed and that you needed to keep an eye on me?' Not that she'd been dead tired, hungry and had basically passed out from that one glass of champagne.

'It seemed the logical conclusion.' He shrugged with a helpless gesture. But he was so not helpless, he was so very powerful. 'You fell asleep before I could get your address from you,' he added. 'Though I tried to wake you.'

'Oh?' She tried to act cool by casually perching on one of the kitchen stools and avoiding eye contact again. 'How did you try?'

Had it been with a kiss?

Well, duh, of course not. If he'd kissed her again, she'd *definitely* have woken. And if he'd kissed her again…? Her mind tracked back to that moment by the lake last night. That sensation rushed in, curling her toes, cooking her from the inside out. But she drew a sharp breath. She *wasn't* going to mention it. Not to him. Not to anyone. She was only going to remember it when she was all by herself and she'd *never* admit that she was going to treasure it always. While she'd vowed to be honest, there were some things he didn't need to know. He was already arrogant enough.

But then she looked at him and her belly flipped.

He knew anyway, didn't he? He was watching her, his eyes darkening with that wicked gleam of intent. He knew what she was thinking about and he knew how much he affected her. She'd even bet he knew just how much she wanted him to kiss her again. Right now.

Rafe studied Grace for another moment, waiting for her to fill the silence the way any other woman would have already. Was she really going to walk out of here without addressing that kiss? Even when it was clear from her expression that she wanted another?

Yes, it seemed she was. She'd tried to sneak out without saying goodbye—a walking mess of embarrassment. There was no way that kiss was going to be the only one they shared. But he whirled away from her and snatched up a few tissues to press to the wound on her hand. He'd give her time and draw her in.

'How's your knee this morning?' he asked, hiding the fact he felt more invigorated than he'd felt in far too long.

'A bit sore and bruised but it's fine.'

He nodded. 'Hold this and give me a moment, I need to find the first-aid kit.' He began opening cupboards in the butler's kitchen. 'I'm still finding my way around.'

'You bought the place furnished?' She appeared in the open doorway and looked at the working pantry with wide eyes.

'There was some furniture, I believe. Then one of my staff fitted it out with a few essentials after the restoration work was completed.' He'd deliberately not come to see it before the work was done. He'd wanted it perfect.

'A few essentials?' She marvelled with a soft laugh as she studied the chrome coffee machine that wouldn't look out of place in a restaurant. She walked over and ran a finger along the smooth, gleaming machine and pinned him with that wide, expressive gaze. 'Do you even know how to use it?'

There was no hiding the edge of judgement in her query.

'You'd be amazed by the number of things I know how to use,' he drawled, not telling her he'd already made himself a coffee over an hour ago while he'd been pacing the place, waiting for her to wake up. Opening another cupboard, he pounced on a red box with the words 'First Aid' emblazoned across the top. Perfect.

'I can't imagine buying a house without having seen it. Do you do that often?'

He glanced at her and saw the amusement dancing in her eyes. He turned back to sift through the selection of plasters. 'I have a number of properties.'

'Properties?' She faced him, that unrepentantly joyous laughter in her voice again. 'They're hardly the same as a *home*.'

He had no need for a home. He needed only space and comfort and a decent bed, and frankly he could get that anywhere. Ideally a hotel with all those extra features, like food on call. *Properties*, on the other hand, were business. A way to build his empire and the security and success he enjoyed.

'How many properties do you have?' he asked acidly.

'I own none as yet, but I only want one *home*. Definitely only need *one*. I have no desire to trot around the globe.'

'No? Not even in a private jet?' He played up to her pious little performance. 'Maybe you should try it sometime. You might find it's not so bad.'

'And isolate myself completely from the rest of the world?' She shook her head. 'I actually want to *know* my neighbours. Not keep them out with my fancy gates and scary beeping security system and private transport.'

'You want to know them?' He shuddered theatrically and fished a tube of antiseptic ointment from the box as well as a plaster.

She waggled her finger at him and laughed softly. 'You make out you want your space and privacy but you *chose* to go to that party last night.'

'I needed to promote my interests—namely this villa—and I might have learned something interesting.'

She blinked at him. 'You didn't talk to any of them to learn anything.'

'That's because I was distracted.' He was distracted again now—by her eyes, her lips and the raging desire that had meant he'd hardly slept.

'You *wanted* to be distracted. That's why you took me with you. You used me to avoid everyone else. What I still don't understand is why you wanted to go in the first place.'

The truth was banal. 'Because I could.' He smiled. He hadn't been allowed here years ago. Now there was no stopping him. 'And *you* used me to get an up-close look at the *palazzo*. I say we're even,' he said firmly. 'Now, be quiet and let me fix this.'

He carefully cleaned her wound and dabbed on the antiseptic ointment but her question had opened up that old wound and the memories scurried.

All his childhood he'd been told of the beautiful Villa Rosetta, the holiday home his father lived in for a few months each year. But by the time Rafe had arrived, his father was too ill to visit. When he'd died, it had been ruled out altogether. His half-brother, his nephew held all the power. Leonard and Maurice had laughed at him when he'd asked if he could visit Italy. They'd said no, just as they'd said no to all his most personal requests.

Including the ones to see his mother.

As a youngster he'd done everything they'd asked of him. His academic achievements had been outstanding, as had his sporting ones. He'd done everything and anything he could to win their attention, to earn the visit from his mother that they'd promised.

It had never happened. And by the time he'd been old enough to make the journey himself, it had been too late.

But in the end he'd learned that winning had some benefits. He garnered attention from *others*—those who sought his advice, strove to emulate his success, trusted him with their assets and made his business even more successful. And it brought him women. Women liked men with money, men who were fit, men who were winners. Once he'd begun winning, he'd won more—a snowball of success after success after success.

But he knew that without the success, without the money, the properties, the physique...they wouldn't want to know him. Just as they hadn't wanted to know him before he'd acquired all those things. So he didn't allow people to get close. He didn't trust anyone and he'd never give a person a chance to reject him, or to betray him, again. He'd had enough of that for a lifetime.

'You're looking very stern. You think it's fatal?' Grace said quietly.

He glanced up into those melted-caramel eyes and forgot to breathe. The hard knot tightening his chest softened—while another part of him altogether hardened to the point of pain. 'I'm resisting the urge to kiss it better,' he replied bluntly.

Her eyes widened. Yeah, he'd win now too—here, with her. He pressed the plaster over her small wound and shot her a speaking look before turning his attention to the coffee machine she'd doubted he could master. Efficiently, ruthlessly, silently proving a point. Doing it all on his own—as always. His terms. His timelines. 'Do you take milk?' he asked.

'No, thank you. I like it strong.'

He bit back the smile at her innocently uttered innuendo and handed her the cup. He watched her sip gratefully. She was clearly starving. 'You're sure about something to eat? I think there might be some pastries in the freezer.'

She half snorted on her next sip of coffee. 'Freezer?' She shook her head and coughed her way back to recovery. 'No, thank you.'

'You don't love frozen pastries?' He laughed ruefully. 'I haven't been into the village yet.'

'You do your own shopping? How arduous for

you,' she teased. 'No, thank you. I'll eat at work—which is at the local bakery, and that's why I need to leave. I should have left half an hour ago.'

She'd told him last night that she was a waitress. No wonder she thought she knew how to make a coffee.

A second later she put the cup on the bench and stood. 'Thanks so much,' she said again. 'But I really need to go or I'll be even more late for work.'

'I'll give you a lift.'

She shook her head. 'I'll bike back. That's how I got here yesterday.'

He walked with her back out to the garden and picked a couple of roses, grinning when she narrowed her eyes at how easily he snapped them from the plant. 'It's all in the angle,' he explained soothingly as he held them out to her. 'Take them to Alex.'

As she took them, she looked right at him and smiled. The pleasure and appreciation in her eyes walloped him in the solar plexus. Suddenly he didn't want her to leave at all. But she was already walking away.

'Thank you. Yet again. I'd better get going.' She glanced back at the villa. 'I guess all those models will be arriving soon?'

Hell, he'd forgotten about that. 'I guess so.' He walked with her up the long driveway. 'The spread will be a good advertisement for the villa.'

'Does it need to be advertised?'

'It's a high-end fashion magazine with extremely discerning readers. Readers who can afford to rent a villa for several thousand a week.' He slowed as they neared the security gates.

'And wear white designer dresses without worrying about spilling stuff on them.' She nodded. 'So you're going to keep it as a holiday home for the super-wealthy?'

'What else?'

'A home,' she said softly.

'No one could live here permanently, they'd never get any work done,' he scoffed, then frowned as he saw something that vaguely resembled a bicycle stashed beside one of the trees. He stepped closer to study it. 'You ride this thing? It's a man's bike. Is it even roadworthy?'

'It's vintage.'

He frowned. 'It sure is something.' An old man's bike. He felt a tightening in his chest but he couldn't hold back his curiosity. 'The same owner as your watch?' Who was the old guy who gave her these things?

'Different. Alex loaned it to me. He's taken care of it for years and it goes like a dream. By that I mean it's fast.'

'You like fast?' he jeered softly. 'I wasn't sure.'

'I like fast. But I also like reliable. Not everyone is all about buying new things, only to discard them after using them once.' She lifted her chin in the air.

'Ouch.' He pressed his hand to his heart, wincing. 'I think the rose has thorns.'

'Roses generally do.' She placed the two she was holding into the pannier at the back of her bicycle. 'Thank you for an interesting evening,' she said awkwardly, glancing up at him when she was done.

He knew he was standing too close, too much in her way, but he couldn't tear himself away from her. 'It was merely interesting?'

She nodded slowly, her caramel gaze not leaving his. She didn't seem to be breathing. Her focus strayed to his lips. She was remembering—he was instinctively certain—remembering every moment of that scorching kiss. He smiled tightly at the strength of attraction flowing between them. Using an intense amount of self-control, he deliberately stepped back so he no longer blocked her path. After a tiny hesitation she mounted the bike.

'Travel safe,' he called gently as she wobbled her way out of the gates.

He refused to say goodbye. Because he'd have his trespassing tourist back in his villa soon enough. But next time she'd be in his bed and wide, wide awake.

CHAPTER FIVE

GRACIE PUSHED THE fierce surge of energy from her body, pedalling so fast the usual fifteen-minute trip took only nine. She whipped upstairs to her apartment to quickly shower and change. She'd be only a few minutes late to the *pasticceria*, but on her way back out she nearly tripped over the elderly man checking the tires on her bike.

'Alex.' She smiled warmly, pleased to see him looking a bit better. But immediately she reproached him. 'Why are you up and about so early?'

'Your light battery is almost flat,' he said gruffly.

'You should still be in bed, recuperating.'

'I wanted to see you.' His eyes had a little of their usual sparkle back.

'To find out about your roses?' she teased. 'Here.' Gracie lifted the fresh-picked blooms from the basket. 'They're perfect, as you can see.'

'I can.' His hand shook slightly as he took them but he wasn't studying the roses as much as he was scrutinising her.

'You really should go back inside and rest.' Gracie put her hands on her hips.

'Stop fussing. Sofia was here half the night, fussing.' He hesitated and finally looked down at the blooms in his hand. 'You enjoyed the fireworks?'

'I did,' she said, instinctively wary.

'I didn't hear you come home last night. I wasn't sure…'

Gracie smiled even as she blushed with embarrassment. At least she had someone in her life who cared about her. And that was nice. 'It was a late night. I ended up staying at a friend's house.'

There was a twinkle in Alex's eye. 'Sofia's niece Stella swung by after the fireworks and showed us some photos from the *palazzo*'s event on her phone.'

Photos? Gracie had forgotten that people might've taken pictures.

'You went to the *palazzo* for the festival.' Alex finally got to his point.

'Yes.' She abandoned any fleeting hope of keeping her exact whereabouts secret. 'I met the villa's owner when watering the roses and he invited me. I could hardly say no to the chance to get inside the *palazzo*.'

'Of course not.' Alex's expression sharpened. 'Was he nice?'

Gracie wasn't entirely sure that 'nice' was the best adjective to describe Rafael, but it would do. 'He seemed to be.'

'So my roses will be safe.'

Gracie laughed. 'He'd be crazy to touch them. I think he's all about preserving his assets and he knows their value.'

'I guess that's good.' But the old man didn't smile. 'Could you check on them again tonight, please? It's going to be even hotter today.'

'Are you sure you need me to?' Gracie was mortified at the thought of going back there. Rafael would assume she'd become another of his 'stalkers'.

'Yes.' Alex sat down heavily in his outdoor seat by his container garden and coughed a couple of times. 'I really appreciate your help on this, Gracie,' he wheezed. 'It doesn't take much for them to dehydrate.'

She narrowed her gaze but as he peered up at her she sighed. Alex was incorrigible, but she was fond of him and now he'd taken a seat she could see he was truly struggling for breath. He was the first and best friend she'd made here, and she'd do anything for him.

Rafael couldn't get away from the villa fast enough. Overrun with leggy models, make-up artists, the photographer and his many intrusive assistants, his quiet had been shattered. Worse was the lingering thread of temptation that Grace had left—unravelling the last peace left in his mind. And he couldn't help but agree with her assertion that pastries were better fresh, not frozen. It took only an hour of noisy distraction and interruption from all the officious assistants before he gave in and drove to Bellezzo.

It wasn't the largest village—merely a haphazard collection of old buildings clinging to the hillside right on the lakefront. According to the boundary sign, it had a population of just under six hundred people and apparently every last one of them was currently queuing in the town's only *pasticceria*. It was a bar, bakery and café all bundled into one small shop on the corner of the central square. After parking the car, he glimpsed a familiar ancient bike propped against the wall of the alley next door but the delicious smell propelled him into the tiny café itself. He paused in the doorway, blinking at the number of people waiting to be served, all apparently unfazed by the length of the queue. The pastries had to be stellar because it wasn't just tourists queuing, but locals as well. He couldn't see through the crowd to scope the food in cabinets, but he could see above them to the staff behind the counter.

Grace's hair was swept back in a neat braid and that fresh, sparkling smile was on her lips as she expertly filled delicate-looking pastries. She wasn't serving but *baking*. As she worked, she helped the tourists who spoke little Italian with their orders—translating, interpreting, laughing. It was crowded and busy and looked and smelled insanely delicious. His stomach growled.

'I need another dozen, Gracie,' an older Italian woman, clearly the boss, called.

'On it.'

Gracie. It suited her. He ignored the curious glances of other customers and watched her work. Everyone watching was salivating, including him. But he had some other reactions that weren't anywhere near as appropriate for a public place. Breathing out, he rested his eyes by looking around. There were a few small tables crammed inside—all occupied by satisfied customers drinking coffee and eating. A few more were leaning against a tall counter.

Pictures of the lake hung on the walls, a few signs advertised the specials of the day—it seemed the place opened till lunch and then opened again at night for coffee and pizza. A couple of newer-looking signs advertised their catering service and also picnic packing for those hiring boats for a float on the lake. Clearly the business was aiming to make the most of the summer season and the influx of people.

He glanced again at the queue ahead of him. A couple of guys—clearly tourists—were watching Grace with the same kind of hunger he was desperately trying to suppress.

She was so skilled he knew she'd had serious training. After another two trays were done, she helped serve.

Rafael watched with increasing dismay as the pastry cabinet was depleted by the million customers ahead of him. His mouth was watering and his stomach was rumbling worse than hers had been first thing this morning. But worse was the thrum of blood beating around his body. Finally he got to the front—and met her gaze.

'Oh.'

Rafe smiled at the flush that immediately mottled her skin.

'I really need food,' he all but begged her before she could speak. 'Enough for me and those fashion-shoot people.'

'Fashion-shoot people?' Her eyebrows lifted sceptically. 'I didn't think models ate anything... I definitely wouldn't have thought they'd eat pastries filled with custard and cream.'

'These pastries would tempt *anyone*.' He was dying of hunger. For everything. Recklessness fired in his blood. 'You made them. You're the temptress.'

That colour built in her cheeks again, but before she could speak, he put in another plea. 'They're going fast. I really don't want to miss out.'

'We always sell out before lunchtime.'

'I'm not surprised.' He smiled at the pride in her voice.

'You'd like a selection?'

Right now he'd take anything she cared to toss his way. 'Enough for nine people. And me.'

'You have a particularly large appetite?' A mischievous smile tugged the corners of her mouth.

Was she flirting with him?

'I'd call it healthy.' He watched her lift the pastries into a large box. 'Did you give Alex the roses?'

'Yes, thank you.' Her smile bloomed to one of true delight. 'He was satisfied with their condition.' She bit her lip as she closed the lid of the box. 'I think he was worried you're going to rip them out.'

'Why would I do that?' He was taken aback. 'I like beautiful things.'

She laughed. 'You like to collect them.'

He wasn't going to deny it, neither was he going to apologise for the fact. 'Who doesn't like spending time with beauty?' He wanted lots of time with her. 'Beauty and her roses.'

She carefully put a sticker on the box to secure the lid. 'You don't need to try so hard,' she said so quietly he leaned closer to hear. 'You know you'd only have to crook your little finger.'

He was so staggered by the fierce satisfaction her unsolicited admission gave him he actually put a hand on the counter to steady himself. 'Actually, I didn't know that.' He waited for her to look at him again. 'You just don't do anything the way I expect.'

'Don't I?'

'You're unpredictable. Definitely not like any other women I've met.'

'You've met many and they're all predictable?' She looked at him with such disappointment.

'Not gonna lie.' He grinned unashamedly. 'What is it that's made you so different?'

She pushed the box on the counter towards him and whispered conspiratorially, 'I didn't have a normal childhood.'

'Now, that *is* predictable.' He laughed. 'Because who does?'

She smiled brightly and nudged the box another inch towards him. 'Here you go.'

'Thank you,' he said.

'Have a great day,' she said brightly.

He smiled as he scooped up the box of deliciousness. 'Oh, I intend to.'

Have a great day? Did she think she was working in some giant fast-food company? Did she think she could actually flirt with the guy and get somewhere? Had she really just told him, *You'd only have to crook your little finger*?

Why had she said that? Why did her brain go AWOL the second he appeared?

And all that he'd done in response was to walk out without a backwards glance.

The fizz of electricity she'd felt on seeing him again was now snuffed out as she remembered just what Rafael Vitale had planned for his day—models, pastries, sunshine, models…all at a beautiful lakeside villa with an infinity pool and an award-winning heritage garden…and had she mentioned *models*?

Of *course* he was going to have the best day ever. And her involvement in it was over already. He might've kissed her last night but it had probably been out of boredom. Then she'd made a fool of herself by falling asleep on him and followed it up with another trivial medical issue this morning. He'd made no attempt to kiss her again. Now she'd just admitted she fancied him and he'd walked out.

'Are you okay, Gracie?' Francesca interrupted her thoughts. 'I need you to—'

'I know, I'm on it. Sorry.'

Francesca's smile widened. 'Who was he?'

'No one.' Gracie sighed. And she never wanted to see him again, right?

She'd have to tell Alex he needed to check on the roses himself tonight. She wasn't going near the Villa Rosetta ever again.

Eight hours later she quickly walked along the curved, crossing paths of the stunning villa gardens, cursing Alex beneath her breath. He'd played the invalid card again at lunchtime and begged her to water the roses. Fortunately for him it was her other night off the evening shift at the *pasticceria*, so she could do this. But it was only for him. And this was absolutely the last time.

She'd biked slowly because it was still hot and because she really didn't want to be seen by anyone. The place was probably still overrun with models. They'd probably have moved on from photos to frolicking—and it was too awkward. But when she'd walked down the driveway, the air was still and the villa grounds silent. Perhaps they'd all gone out on the lake? She got the hose out and swiftly started watering the beautiful plants.

'I was hoping you'd come.'

He was behind her, sneaking up in that impossibly silent way of his. But she switched the hose off before turning this time—refusing to make that mistake again, refusing to blush at the juvenile double entendre her one-track mind read into his statement. But she failed on that second one. 'Rafael.'

For some reason the guy was barefoot, yet he was still intimidatingly tall. Slacks, a white shirt, the sleeves rolled back to reveal tanned, muscular forearms.

'Call me Rafe, Gracie.' He glanced at the hose

she still held. 'Why isn't it on an automated hydration system?'

She swallowed, flustered by the way the intimate version of her name rolled off his tongue so easily. 'Alex likes to do things slowly and properly. By hand. He likes to check on every plant every day.' She glanced behind him to the villa—still and silent. Unfortunately, *she* could be neither still nor silent. She fidgeted. 'The photo shoot is over?'

'Yes. They've returned to Milan.'

'And you're not having an orgy with all the models?' The stupid question slipped out before she could stop it.

'It's a nice idea but wasn't my preference for tonight.' His wicked grin flashed. 'Sorry to disappoint.'

Oh, she wasn't disappointed and she couldn't help smiling. Her heart rate wouldn't settle and he closed the gap until he was right in front of her.

'What?' she asked, suddenly wary.

'I'm not sure if you remember, but you kissed me last night. I was hoping you might do it again.'

Shock impacted her body. Remembrance of that kiss—she'd been trying not to think of it.

'I kissed you?' She was stunned by his interpretation of events.

'Yes.' His sudden smile was unnervingly boyish. 'I liked it.'

She stared, now speechless. But the rest of her

reacted intensely. Sensation ignited deep in her muscles, rendering it impossible for her to remain still.

'I thought you might appreciate my honesty,' he added simply. 'Did you even remember that we kissed?'

'I didn't hit my head.' She breathlessly backed up a pace. 'I hadn't forgotten.'

'But you didn't say anything.'

'Neither did you.'

There was a long moment of silence when she couldn't think what to say, she was so surprised. He simply looked at her, and the longer he looked at her, the warmer she became, the more tense. The more...*wanting*.

'Do you think you'd consider kissing me again?' he finally asked quietly. 'I've been hoping you will. I haven't been able to think about anything else all day.'

His statement shocked her so much she spoke before thinking. 'Not even with all those models here to distract you?'

'I don't give a damn about any models. I just want you.'

His vehemence rendered her immobile. Intensity flared as all the memories she'd tried so hard to suppress all day came fizzing back.

'If I kiss you again, will you kiss me back?' she whispered.

'Count on it.'

She couldn't hold back her smile. 'What else will you do?'

'Anything you'll allow me to.' He cocked his head and looked at her with those wicked, experienced eyes. 'Ideally everything.'

Fire flickered along her veins. He'd just promised her everything she'd never had. All she had to do was reach out and take it. And that reckless part of her now took control.

'Come closer so I can kiss you, then,' she commanded huskily.

Arrogant pleasure gleamed in his eyes as he obediently stepped nearer. But any sense of her being the boss in this was laughable. She was like a puppet on a string—he'd pulled her to do as he'd wanted. But *she* wanted it too. And she'd have it—him. She'd be mad not to.

She rose on tiptoe and brushed her lips against his. True to his word, he kissed her back. But it was a feather-light kiss, as if he was afraid she might step away at any moment. She had no intention of doing any such thing. She crept closer, throwing the hose to the ground so she could wrap her arms around his neck. The second she did that, he slid his arms around her waist and drew her against him. Her lips parted in pleasure at the press of his body and he took advantage, stroking into her mouth, lusciously deepening the kiss.

She was instantly lost—spilling straight back into that overwhelming spell he'd cast over her last night. So the fizzing she'd felt in every cell hadn't been from the champagne? This instant, incandescent response hadn't been a dream?

No. Being kissed by Rafael Vitale was categorically the most pleasurable experience of her life. She didn't want him ever to stop. Her body was somehow so boneless she had to lean against his hard muscles…tripping easily to absolute acquiescence. With seemingly superhuman strength he kept kissing her while actually lifting her—up and then down to the close-cropped, perfect grass. He tumbled her back and knelt over her, his hands loosening her hair, freeing every last one of her inhibitions in seconds.

He sat back a second to wrench his T off and she simply stared at his beauty and inhaled that delicious woodsy scent of him. What with the grass, the roses, the sweet summer heat…she didn't need champagne to make her giddy. She just needed him. He paused for the merest moment, his eye catching hers, and his low laugh was wicked and knowing.

She had no chance to reply. He rained kisses across her face and jaw, his hands stroking—deftly, softly, surely. She shivered with pleasure as she felt the warmth of the late sun on her skin… vaguely registering that her blouse was unbuttoned and her breasts unfettered because her bra was already undone… In moments both items were scattered either side of them. So the man knew how to get a girl out of her clothes? Fantastic. That was just…fantastic.

He reached up and snapped a large rose from the bush beside them and shook it so the petals fell like sweet-scented snowflakes—showering her with soft pieces of scented silk. Playful and spontaneous and strong, he swept her along with his swift seduction. She smiled blindly as he bent his head and fastened his hot mouth around her tightly budded nipple and tugged—shooting a flame of pure eroticism deep into her belly. At the force of it she moaned, her hips instinctively lifting.

'Beauty and her roses.' He rolled a petal against her skin. 'I want *your* fireworks tonight, Gracie.'

Given her body was three steps ahead of her brain, it seemed that wasn't going to be a problem.

'But I like to do things properly too,' he added, lifting his head to catch her eyes with his dark, glinting gaze. 'Slowly and by hand.' He slid his palm beneath her skirt and pushed it up.

Gracie could barely breathe as the sensation of warm air brushed her thighs and she watched him lower his shockingly handsome face towards an even more shocking destination. Was she going to let him…?

*Yes…*yes, she was. Because suddenly she didn't

want slow. She didn't want gentle. She just wanted it all. Now.

'There's something to be said for fast.' She quivered at the light rasping heat of his stubble on her thighs.

'Not in this instance.'

But there was no stopping the soaring sensations he was stirring so easily within her. With the heat and the scent and the power of him, every touch sent her further toward the fire. Breathless, restless, she rocked her hips, meeting the slide of his fingers and brush of his lips. As his kiss breached the barrier of her panties, she bucked involuntarily, a pure, instinctive response.

'*Oh...*' She arched, a length of pure tension. '*Rafe!*'

With only one more touch, unbearably good sensations streamed from cell to cell until her whole pleasure-starved body was alight with wanton, wonderful joy. She cried out in pure rapture as spasms of ecstasy shook her again and again and again, powerfully pulsing until they slowly gentled and ebbed, leaving her speechless, boneless and completely blissed out.

'*Caramellina,*' he chided softly, sprawling across her legs to hold her in place beneath him. 'Too quick.' His laughter was low and sexy.

Dazed, Gracie opened her eyes and looked straight into his. She saw the humour there, together with the smug satisfaction she knew he felt from pleasing her 'too quick'. But she also saw his hunger. Delicious anticipation rippled through her as she watched the appetite in his eyes darken and grow. What exactly would he want now? The thought of doing to him what he'd done to her made mini-bursts of bliss shudder down her spine. The thought of letting him do more made her hotter still in that secret part of her that he'd just searched out.

Two internal forces powerfully buffeted her soul—gratitude and greed. She adored what he'd just done to her, and now she wanted more. She wanted it *all*.

She knew this meant nothing to him. It was nothing more than a pleasurable moment on a sunny, summery afternoon. For her it was more—it was a *chance*. Here. Now. She wanted everything he had to offer. It was, she knew, all he *could* and would ever offer her, and that was just fine. But he'd been honest with her and she had to offer him the same.

'There's something you should know,' she babbled quickly before she could chicken out. 'I haven't done this before.'

He stilled. 'Done what—had sex outdoors in the late afternoon?'

'None of it,' she breathed quickly. 'Not in the late afternoon. Not outdoors. Not at all.'

CHAPTER SIX

Rafe stared at her. 'You're a…'

'Virgin. Yes.' Gracie suddenly chuckled as he stumbled on the word. 'Not…done this. Ever. Not had anyone do that before either.' She confessed it all with a mortified smile.

But she wanted to. She wanted everything. She'd just let him do something so intimate and now she wanted him to do everything else. 'I'm not telling you because I wanted you to stop. I'm telling you because… I thought you should know. In case it makes a difference.'

He was staring at her like she was suddenly an alien species. 'As to whether you lose it here on the grass in a quickie?'

'I like it on the grass,' she confessed boldly, because now she had nothing else left to lose. 'It's warm and it smells nice and it feels free. And I don't mind quick, if that's all you can offer.'

A startled look widened his eyes and he suddenly laughed. Then he leaned closer to brush a lock of her hair back from her face. 'How is it possible you're still a virgin?'

She was just appallingly glad he was back in kissing range. 'What do you mean, "How is it possible"?'

'You're…' He paused, his gaze holding hers.

'What?'

'A natural.'

'Is that good?'

'Yes.'

'So don't stop,' she whispered.

To her immense pleasure, he leaned closer still. But it wasn't to touch her, it was to speak softly. 'Why are you going to throw away something that's obviously important to you on a guy you've only just met? Why would you want to do that?'

'What makes you think it's important to me? It's just that I was never in the position to do this before now. This is just good timing. Finally.'

'Wow. Lucky me,' he said dryly. 'Be more honest. Say the rest. If you trust me enough to tell me you want to give your virginity to me, then go all the way and tell me *why*.'

Trust him to challenge her, the guy wasn't just sharp looking. She drew in a breath and braved up enough to talk. 'I've been running for a long time. Like, a *long* time. Now I'm finally in a place I want to stay and I'm happy and what I thought I wanted all that time is no longer the same. Before I didn't want to give it up easily. I thought I wanted it to mean something.'

'Mean something like what?' His expression froze. 'True love?'

She giggled. 'I really wish you could see the look on your face right now.'

'Are you having me on?'

'No, I'm actually telling you the truth, you're just not listening to the important part. I *am* honest.' She shrugged. 'I lied about *everything* when I was younger and it's not something I want to do any more. Who I was. Where I was from. What my name was.'

'Just the little things.' His gaze narrowed. 'Why?'

Maybe it was the post-orgasmic high. Maybe it was the cocoon of his arms. Maybe it was because she'd already crossed so many lines, what did another matter? Maybe it was because she fully believed that the truth would set her free.

'My parents split up when I was seven,' she said softly. 'They had custody issues and it got really bitter. In the end my mother kidnapped me and we spent twelve years moving every few months to escape him.'

Rafe's jaw dropped and his arms tightened.

'She was terrified an extraction team would get me.' She rushed to explain it quickly. 'So I was educated at our various homes on and off for years. For short bursts I went to actual schools. We went as far away as possible and we were never in one place for long.'

The expression in his eyes had softened. 'You must have been terrified.'

'All the time. My mother did what she thought was best. My father kept fighting to find me.'

'So what happened? Did you ever see your dad? Did your mother get charged? How is it now?'

'Complicated.' She threw him a little smile. 'I grew up—old enough to make my own decisions. I told Mum I wanted to go back. So I did, alone, and I convinced my father not to press charges against her.'

Rafe's gaze narrowed. 'He agreed to that?'

She nodded. She'd lived with him for over a year. She'd tried to fit in with his new family. She'd tried to please them all.

'Look, it happened and I can't go back and change it,' she said firmly. 'I can only move forward and make sure I get what I want now.'

'And what's that?'

She hesitated, afraid her talking too much was just putting him off. But he was still very close, his gaze very direct. So she caved.

'To be secure,' she answered. 'I just want a home.'

'And you've chosen Bellezzo?'

'Why not?' She shrugged. 'It's beautiful, it's warm. The food is amazing and the people are nice.'

'But you have no family here.'

'I have friends. I'm building my career. I have permanency.'

He shook his head. 'There's no such thing as permanency. Certainly not in relationships.'

'This is just you warning me again, right? Or trying to scare me off so I'll retract my offer.' She laughed weakly. 'You don't have to. I want marriage one day and I'm not going to apologise for that, but—'

'You want to get married?' he interrupted, looking at her like she was a lunatic. 'Kids? After what your parents put you through?'

'Don't panic,' she said softly. 'I'm not asking *you*. Not kids. Not marriage. This—right here, right now—with you is an *experience* and it's not one I want to deny myself.'

He didn't reply. She saw the conflicting emotions in his eyes and felt the opportunity sliding from her. She suddenly chilled and wrapped her arms across her bare chest.

'Don't you think I can handle it?' she asked in a small voice.

'No, I don't know that you can.'

'But you shouldn't get to make that choice,' she argued fiercely. '*I* should. This is my body and I know what I can handle. You'd be surprised at what I've already handled.'

He gazed down at her. 'Don't think I underestimate you.'

'Then don't doubt my ability to make this decision.'

'And it's not a rash decision in the heat of the moment?'

'Of course it is.' She couldn't help but laugh. 'But what's wrong with that? I'm actually feeling a moment and that's a good thing and, no, I'm not going to regret it.'

She shifted a little beneath him, unable to resist the urge to move. He was still with her. Still touching her. She could feel the tension within him—he was so very strong, so very skilled. And she had nothing left to lose.

'You're a good kisser,' she said dreamily. I think you'll make it good for me. I deserve good when I've waited so long.'

He rubbed his hand across his jaw but failed to hide his smile. 'I'm a good kisser?'

'Really good.' She nodded.

Despite his obvious arousal, he was still resisting. Her frustration rose.

'It's just lust, right? And doesn't lust fade once you've done it?' she asked. 'Isn't it all in the anticipation? The unknown? And once you've had it, you know, and so it's less of a need. Like my most indulgent pastries. People don't come back for seconds. They're a treat you try just the once.'

He shook his head slowly, not lifting his gaze from hers. 'I saw the queue in your shop today. People do come back for seconds.'

'Okay, maybe seconds.' She giggled. 'But not tenths.'

'You're saying I'm your treat?'

'Yes,' she admitted. 'Life is precious, right? It's quick. You can lose whole chunks without realising. It should have moments of wild amazingness. Isn't this one of those moments?'

'Wild amazingness?'

'And freedom.' She nodded defiantly. 'Yes. Why don't *you* be honest about why you're hesitating? If you don't want to, you don't want to. Don't soften the blow, just say no.' She pushed him but he didn't move.

He ground closer and she inhaled sharply.

'Isn't the virgin thing every man's fantasy?' She grumbled her last-ditch argument.

'*You* are absolutely every man's fantasy, "virgin thing" or not. And I do want to,' he growled back. 'Just you. Just now.'

'Why?' She suddenly challenged him, her heart thudding. 'You wanted honesty from me, I demand the same.'

He looked her in the eye. 'You make me laugh.'

'Really?' She tried to wriggle away from under him. 'I'm your jester?'

To her annoyance he actually laughed, but then rolled and held her tightly so she couldn't escape. 'I enjoy spending time with you. I enjoy looking at you. You feel amazing in my arms and I know

I'll love making you feel pleasure. I won't stop until you do.'

A wave of heat rolled over her—pure anticipation.

'That's what I want most of all,' he added gruffly, grinding down and making her innards quake. 'I know I can. I already have.' He groaned and leant close so his lips brushed hers as he spoke. 'I can't hold off any longer anyway.'

Her lips parted and he plundered. Sensation overwhelmed her. Relieved at his agreement and relishing what was to come, she kissed him back as passionately as she knew how. But to her dismay he suddenly tore away from her.

'Stop playing with me,' she muttered harshly, hurt that she'd thought he'd said yes and was now kneeling three feet away.

'I should.' He sent her a look. 'But I can't.' He dug into his pocket with a vicious movement. 'You hadn't thought about this?' He held up the square foil package. 'We can be wild, but we're not going to be stupid.'

She stared at it, confused.

'I saw you from the villa and brought it with me,' he explained, misconstruing her nonplussed look.

A split second later she realised what it actually was. 'Were you determined or hopeful?' she asked with a smile as she watched him shuck the rest of his clothes and tear open the condom packet.

'Both. Same as you.'

His growl made her giggle—that and her nerves. 'You made me answer all those questions when you had already decided?' she asked with mock-outrage.

'I was decided up until you dropped the V-bomb on me,' he muttered.

She didn't answer because now he was naked and she was speechless. He was *magnificent*—broad-shouldered and slim-hipped with muscles everywhere in between, and at the apex of his athletic legs?

Awestruck, she watched, stilled and silenced, as he sheathed himself.

Oh, my. Oh, my. Oh, my.

He glanced up and caught her staring with her mouth ajar. A shamelessly wicked grin curved his mouth. A split second later he pounced, tumbling her back onto the grass. She welcomed his dominance, needing his expertise and guidance. Frankly she just needed his touch. He wasn't arguing any more. He was all action and it was exactly what she'd not known she needed until now.

He kissed her until she was breathless and writhing—it took mere moments. Her legs naturally splayed that bit further, her hips restless under his. He laughed as he kissed his way down her body. 'You're not getting it that quickly, Gracie. I intend to take my time with you.'

She didn't want him to take his time—they'd wasted enough of that talking. She just wanted him. He kissed her—long and hard—and she hurtled into that hedonistic heat once more. He was so clever with his touches—hot and skilled and certain. He peeled her skirt and panties down together with torturously slow hands, baring her completely to his gaze, to his touch, to his tongue. He made good use of the access she granted him. She ran her fingers through his hair, holding him closer, savouring the sensations he sparked with every swoop and swish of his fingers... Oh, his *fingers*.

'Rafe...' She gasped as he pressed the tip of one of those wickedly skiiLful fingers into her tight channel. But before she could say more, he slid his tongue across her tiny sensitive nub. Again and again as his finger slipped deeper. It was so sudden. So intense. So *fantastic*.

She started to shake. 'Rafe... I'm going to—'

'I know.' He rose up. 'You're so damn hot, I can't—' He quit talking and kissed her. His tongue plundered her mouth, mimicking the more intimate invasion that she really craved—completely capturing her soul. He kept his hand between her legs, learning her secrets, slipping that one finger in and out, and then two fingers, and now she was so close again her muscles tightened in readiness for impending orgasm.

As she desperately moaned into his mouth, he nudged her legs that bit further apart with his and settled his hips closer. Hot, all-consuming desire fogged everything… She wanted…she didn't know what any more… She wanted him to stop teasing, for him to get closer still. But he kept kissing her, kept touching, flicking his thumb fast and light across her sensitive, slick bud, but he kept that one part of himself she wanted most just out of her reach.

She tore her mouth from his. 'Rafe… *Rafe…*'

Just as that searing tension forced her hips high, he moved his hand to hold her butt and thrust. *Hard.*

She cried out, shock knocking the breath from her lungs. She heard his growl—a low sound of pure masculine pleasure.

He was inside her. He was inside her and he was huge and it was so *hot.*

'Oh…*oh…*' Her breath shuddered as she curled up tight—her fingers into his back, her toes, locking her feminine muscles on him—every bit as hard as she could. He was really there—with her, in her—and it was intense.

His mouth hovered only an inch above hers, but he didn't kiss her. Like her, he was suddenly still. But right where she'd wanted him most.

'Are you okay?' she asked almost feverishly when the silence stretched. She was desperate for him to move, for him to kiss her again, to touch her because she was still so close—

'I think I'm supposed to ask you that.' His smile was tight.

'You're not breathing.' But, then, neither was she. She was suspended in a moment of stilled sensation and all she wanted was to tip over into the goodness she knew he had waiting for her.

'I'm trying to stay in control.' He smiled but his teeth were gritted.

'What'll happen if you don't?'

'This'll be over too soon and you won't get the experience you deserve.' He groaned and leaned in to offer a full, carnal kiss. 'The trouble is you feel far, far too good.'

'Yes. I feel good. So good.' She nodded, lifting to catch his lips. 'Yes.'

He gave in to her request and kissed her again, taking his time to explore her thoroughly. *Yes.* That was what she'd wanted. Kisses. Caresses. And as he stroked, her body softened and somehow he slid deeper into her. She gasped again. But now he wasn't still. Now he was moving—his hand cupped her breast, his thumb teased her tight nipple, his lips now nibbled at that tender, sensitive side of her neck, and his hips moved in a sure, slow rhythm— back and forth and back and forth, and her body heated, slickened, adjusting to his even more, and it was so very hot she felt incandescent with need.

He rose up, securing himself with one hand on the grass, while he swept the other along her hip and then inwards. His unerring fingers found their quarry, stroking between them, to tease where he'd teased before—right where she needed it. She breathed in sharply, catching the warm scent of crushed roses and cut grass. The blue skies and sunshine were brilliant but her vision was blinkered—she could see only him, feel only him. The best sensation of all was the one inside her.

'It's amazing,' she muttered as that desperate tension coiled tightly within her again. 'It's amazing…'

Her breathing quickened. She couldn't cope with the heavenly way he was touching her and kissing her and every time he rocked closer he set off all those little switches inside her. She was so turned on, so wickedly, deliciously *close*.

'It's sex,' he teased, his muscles rippling as he exerted powerful mastery over her body. 'It's supposed to feel good.'

'*This* good?' She panted, gazing up at him with dazed eyes, and ran her hands up his strong forearms, locking onto him. She'd had no idea it could ever be this good. He was gorgeous and strong and she felt hot and feverish and *hungry*. 'I've been missing out…'

'Well, let's make up for that now, shall we?' He rolled his hips and pushed that bit harder and, oh, heavens, it was just enough.

'Oh, *yes*.' She arched as ecstatic delight shivered through her body.

Dimly she heard his muttered oath and he swiftly switched his grip, thrusting close and holding her tightly to him as she convulsed. Euphoria ricocheted throughout her body, twisting and tearing her to ecstatic little pieces.

Slowly the spasms ebbed and that deliciously warm sense of satisfaction spread through her limbs. Finally some semblance of sanity returned.

'Thank you,' she muttered softly.

His jaw clenched. He was still plunged deep inside her in that most intimate, fantastic way and it was still there—that spark that he could so easily ignite into another of those searing, mind-blowing moments. His arms were wrapped around her, holding her against him, and his gaze burned through her, watching every rise and fall of the roller coaster of emotion she was on. He looked purposeful, intense—and hungry. So damned ravenous, she shivered all over again.

'Rafe?'

'I don't think I can hold back any more, Gracie,' he warned with a low growl.

He'd been holding back? Stunned, her breath stalled—but she was also curious—how much more could he possibly have to give?

'Don't hold back.' She arched to welcome him deeper. 'I want you to enjoy this as much as I am.'

His answering laugh was more of a choke. 'Oh, I'm enjoying it all right. It's just that I'm about to lose it completely.'

A wave of emotion clogged her throat, because now she understood how much he'd been focused on ensuring *her* pleasure. That meant so much to her and she trusted him completely. But she saw the strain in his features and she wanted him with her in this—every part of him with every part of her.

Tremulously she smiled up at him. Heartfelt and true her words emerged barely audible. 'Then lose it with me.'

He looked into her eyes and she saw the moment he snapped. A split second later he was gripping her so tightly it was almost painful and his hips bucked. He rammed deeper, faster. With a feral growl he hauled her closer and bore down even harder and heavier. His unleashed pace and intensity unveiled a whole other dimension of it to her. She cried out at the same time he did. It was so powerful that even though he'd gripped her tightly, she had to strengthen her hold on him too. With her arms and body and mouth, she clung, riding with him as he hurtled her straight back up to that stratosphere of delight and sizzling tension. Crushed petals combined with sweat and stuck to them both, filling the balmy air with a sweet-edged scent. Every one of his muscles strained as he pounded into her. Overwhelmed, she arched to meet him push for push, panting in pure ecstasy.

'Yes,' he gritted harshly. 'Yes, Gracie. *Yes.*'

She screamed as he detonated their world. A kaleidoscope of sensation exploded—shooting them together into a tornado of elation.

It was *so* much better than good.

CHAPTER SEVEN

RAFAEL VITALE WANTED to stay right where he was, for ever. Damned if he wasn't utterly amazed. Damned if he wasn't a greedy, selfish man who'd taken what she'd offered and then some. He shouldn't have. He should've stopped the second she'd revealed her startling virginity secret. But he'd had too much of a taste of her.

He'd tried to go slow, to be gentle, but she hadn't been slow or gentle with him. She'd been powerful—responsive, passionate, as strong as she was soft. When he'd lost his head, she'd come with him. It had been a rougher ride than he'd intended. But stalling his own orgasm to past the point of torture so he could revel in her unrestrained response had led to a passionate release he hadn't been able to control. So much faster, so much more physical than he'd planned. Yet it had been the best sex of his very experienced life and listening to her struggle to catch her breath now was intensely satisfying.

He lifted his head—seeing her ravished beauty was nothing short of an onslaught on his soul. She regarded him solemnly, all wide eyes, her lips kiss-swollen parted as she panted raggedly. Her creamy skin was reddened in patches from where his stubble had rasped and from where his teeth had nipped. Her hair was free of that braid and mussed, fragments of crushed petals were stuck to her.

She looked thoroughly well used—and glowing from that surge of electricity that a woman only got from climaxing. And Gracie had come more than once while he'd been locked fast inside her. Sensation rippled out from the base of his spine— pure masculine pleasure and pride. And lust. All over again.

Within the dazed glaze of her warm brown eyes a new awareness flickered. As he studied her, it built—blossoming into a bright sparkle. And then she smiled.

'Can we do that again?' she said.

It was both shy request and husky order—one he had no ability to ignore. Because what should have been impossible was now undeniable. Desire resurged, sizzling him inside out and stiffening every inch of his body. He pulled out of her swiftly and propelled himself to his feet, then reached for her. Hoisting her into his arms, he strode towards the villa.

'Rafe?'

'Shower. Bed,' he said briskly. 'Together. Now.'

'Oh.' That kittenish smile widened. 'Okay.'

But by the time he'd carried her to the master bedroom, his inner alarm bells were back online and ringing hard. The intensity he felt with her wasn't normal. To have taken her in such a risky location? With such speed?

Lust, he rationalised. Just lust.

But she looked so tousled, still dazed, still innocent even as awareness edged into her eyes. He was suddenly concerned for her. He was *not* boyfriend material.

'You understand I don't do relationships, Gracie,' he said, carrying her into the large bathroom and setting her on her feet in the shower space.

She leaned against the back wall and looked at him with that wide-open warmth. 'It was that bad with your parents?' she asked softly.

She'd been disarmingly honest with him.

'My mother was fifty-odd years younger than my father,' he said gruffly, turning to flick on the shower. 'She was the gold-digger who seduced the senile old man for his money and got pregnant to secure the fortune.'

When he turned back, she was still looking at him solemnly. 'That's what people said to you?'

That and far worse. Of course, he was echoing the slurs of others. It was the description of those who'd judged her—and by default how they'd judged him too. 'It doesn't matter what they said.'

'I know how people can bully,' she said. 'Of course it matters.'

He'd been able to handle the words. It had been the actions of bullies that had been worse. And the worst bully of all had been his half-brother.

'And it wasn't true, was it?' she said softly. 'That's why it hurt, because you couldn't defend them. She wasn't a gold-digger, he wasn't senile.'

'Well, she definitely wasn't rich.' He smiled and turned her so he could soap her back. 'And he was old.'

'But they cared about each other?'

'For what good it did them, yes.'

'She made him happy.'

'But the reaction of his older children didn't,' he countered. 'And then they made her life hell.'

'And, by extension, yours?'

He nodded. 'After he died, they sent me away to a school as far away as they could find.' He felt her soften beneath his hands—but he didn't want her pity.

'It wasn't all bad,' he added roughly. 'I learned how to be independent. How to survive, how to succeed.'

'But what happened to your mum?'

He released her. She faced him before he could formulate a deflection.

'She died,' he said baldly.

How was he standing here, completely naked, talking to this woman about something he never discussed with *anyone*? He loathed thinking about it and he certainly never shared it. Certainly not with a one-night stand. Which was *all* this was. But she'd been honest with him and somehow that stuff had just spilled out and the weird thing was he didn't regret it. But he couldn't tell her more—not about his mother.

'I'm sorry.'

'Yeah, well.' He reached past her to turn off the shower. 'It wasn't like you had it that much better.' He still couldn't get over the childhood she'd had. 'How can you still believe that a relationship could ever last?'

'How can you choose to live a life that's so hopeless?'

'Hopeless?' He laughed and draped a towel around her shoulders. 'Because I don't want marriage and two kids?'

'It should be at least four kids,' she told him with a cheeky smile.

'Four?' He shuddered and pulled her into the bedroom. 'And that's how people get *trapped*. They hurt each other because they settle, they stay together too long.'

'That's not why they hurt each other,' she argued. 'People grow and change and sometimes they don't grow together. Sometimes they're scared. Sometimes they're mean. Sometimes they're mean because they're scared.' She shrugged and inadvertently almost lost the towel. 'I sure don't have all the answers, but loss is a part of life,' she said. 'It doesn't mean we give up trying for anything meaningful.'

'No, we don't give up trying for anything en-

joyable. You plan for the end at the beginning.' He walked forward, backing her up to his bed.

'Your short time frames.'

'I've found it's more fun that way—short and sweet. Then there's no confusion.' He gave her a nudge so she fell onto his bed.

Like this, one night. Because never again would he have what was his stolen from him. Never again would he be vulnerable and at the mercy of other people's whims. *He* called the shots. He remained in control. And he'd remain in control now.

To his delight, she didn't just sit on the bed, she lay right back.

'Do you have a contract and everything before you sleep with a woman?' She all but batted her lashes at him.

He laughed, enjoying her teasing and her honesty. 'I don't need to. A conversation is usually sufficient.'

'Is it?' she asked. 'And there are no disappointed, hurt lovers in your past?'

He looked at her, his amusement easing. 'It's not my fault if a woman changes her expectations halfway through. I'm always upfront about what I'm offering.'

'And what you want never changes?'

He shook his head and knelt on the bed. 'I'm very certain about what I want from life.'

'How wonderful for you.' She cupped his jaw. 'I think you're missing out.'

'Says the inexperienced romantic in the room.' He leaned down and kissed her. 'Don't think you can change me, Gracie. That's how some of those women in my past might have been hurt.'

'You're immutable. Got it.' She tilted her chin at him. 'But don't you think you can change me either. I don't need toughening up.' She pressed her fingertip to his chest. 'I'm more resilient than you.'

'How do you figure that?'

'At least I'm not afraid to take a chance on someone. I'm not afraid to put my heart out there.'

He leaned forward, letting her nail press harder into his skin. 'And here's where you discover my secret, Gracie. I don't have a heart.' He refused to *feel* anything there.

'Of course you do,' she scoffed, gently splaying her soft hand right across his ribs, feeling for herself. 'If you didn't have a heart, you wouldn't be alive. You can't hide from being human, you can't always stay safe.'

'I know how to stay safe.' He distracted her with a nip to her neck.

'By keeping yourself busy buying new things? More properties to rattle about in?'

'By keeping myself busy with *all* the things I enjoy. Including this.'

'Well, maybe you should stop talking and get busy again. If you're granting me only a short amount of your amazing company, let's not waste another second.' She whipped the towel off him.

He glowered at her as she laughed up at him. 'You're a brat.'

She only laughed again. 'Oh, no, *you're* the brat. But fortunately for you, you're good at this sex thing. And I want more of it. Now, please.'

It was the 'please' that got him—a little breathless, a hint of shyness beneath that unloaded, simple request. She got what this was and what it wasn't.

He couldn't get close enough, fast enough, couldn't extract enough of those sighs from her. He'd torment her with unbearable pleasure. He was energised to make it even better, wanting to prove to her just how damn good this could be. He'd forget about his own pleasure entirely. Yet it happened anyway—he was the hottest he'd ever been for a woman. And somehow he lost control of the situation all over again. In the friction between them, he burned too hot, too quick, just as she did all over again.

All his intentions blurred as *his* brain scattered. There was only movement, only feeling, only blistering need. Until he felt her trembling and heard her scream as she shuddered in his arms. He clutched her closer and roared in primal satisfaction, his body utterly spent, before the world around him went black.

* * *

Rafe woke slowly, blinking a few times as he registered the pleasant discomfort of his muscles—yet already desire was priming them again, loosening and tightening simultaneously, prepping for a session of slow wake-up sex. He sensed the hour was early—perfect for one last taste before she left. Except it would be unwise. It would be simpler, safer for her to leave without another round, given her inexperience. Yeah, the sooner she left, the better.

His body thought otherwise. With a low, lazy groan he rolled to face her, only to discover she wasn't beside him. He reached over to feel the cool sheet. As he was about to call out, she walked into the room, completely dressed. He stared uncomprehendingly. She'd showered and he hadn't woken?

'Why are you up?' Disappointment washed over him.

'I'm late for work.' She bit her lip but her smile was still radiant. 'I should have left half an hour ago but I'm hoping Francesca won't mind because I came up with the most amazing idea for a new filling overnight.'

He stared at her. She'd been *thinking* overnight? When had she had the time to *think*?

'So I've got to dash but I'm glad you woke up. I didn't want to hunt for paper to leave you a note.'

She'd been going to leave without saying goodbye? She didn't want to stay in bed with him? She wasn't bothered that the night was over?

'That was really, really good. Honestly,' she added in her nonstop way. 'Thank you so much. It was a once-in-a-lifetime amazing experience.'

Her compliment didn't give him the satisfied feeling she doubtless meant it to. Instead, he felt like some stud who'd just got full marks for best in show.

'You're leaving right now?' he growled as she stayed out of kissing reach.

'Yes. There's so much to do at work. I can't let Francesca down.'

Of course she couldn't. 'And you're okay? No regrets?'

'Oh, no, it was amazing.' She fanned her face and smiled that shy yet sassy smile. 'But one night only.' She turned away, nodding furiously as if convincing herself. 'That was your stipulation and I accept that. There's no point in wishing otherwise anyway, that wouldn't be helpful to me.'

She looked beautiful and fresh and horrendously prepared to go to work. How could she think about *anything* other than wanting to get back into bed with him right this second?

'Why wouldn't it be helpful to you?' he asked, surliness curling inside.

Her smile deepened. 'It just wouldn't.'

Here she was happily enforcing *his* rule, but while he'd got what he'd said he wanted, the fact that someone *else* had called it meant he now wanted the exact opposite. And here he was thinking he was so grown-up and over all the denials of his childhood. Back then the second someone had told him he couldn't have something, he'd wanted it, and he'd done whatever it took to get it. But this time was worse than any other. He grabbed her wrist before she could step completely out of reach.

'I'm not able to be as adult as you about this,' he said huskily. 'How's that for some honesty?'

A wary look entered her eyes. 'What do you mean?'

'I mean that while I don't want this to be anything more, I don't want you to go. I don't want you to leave my bed just yet.'

Her smile blossomed, jerking every one of his muscles to stiffer attention. Killing him. But he could feel her pulse skipping faster every second she studied him.

'Thank you for that compliment.' Her voice was a little husky. 'I'm glad you enjoyed it too, but I *really* can't be late,' she said. 'There's too much to do.'

There *was* too much to do—everything with her all over again. He caught her quick glance down his body and he leaned closer. But then she flicked her hand, twisting free of his grip.

'I must go.' She shook her head. 'There are many, so many…other things I have to do. I had this idea and I think it will work…'

He realised, belatedly, that she was breathlessly babbling her way out of his room. Nervous, embarrassed...emotional.

His lovers always said yes to him, always jumped when he asked them to. But not Gracie. She was getting away the only way she knew how, and even though five minutes ago he'd been ready to rush through any awkward goodbye and hustle her out of the house, he now found *her* awkwardness endearing. And at the realisation she was actually leaving, he felt oddly bereft.

'Sorry.' She rushed her words. 'Really do have to run.'

But the parting smile she flashed at him wasn't sorry, it was shy and grateful and he wanted to kiss her. Instead, all he did was blink at the empty doorway.

The silence echoed long after he'd heard the front door close behind her.

He wanted to hear her teasing laugh and turn it into a quivering sigh again. He wanted to see her sweet eyes smoulder with that new awareness. He growled in self-mockery and tossed the sheet from his lazy, lust-aching bones. One night was all he did.

He had the villa. He'd had an immensely satisfying night with a beautiful woman. He had his space.

Now he'd get back to work.

CHAPTER EIGHT

'WE NEED TO make even more tomorrow, but I honestly don't know how we can.' Francesca locked the door and slumped back against it.

They'd sold out at the *pasticceria* before lunchtime, even though Gracie had made a third more pastries than usual.

'I know,' Gracie groaned. 'I'm going to have to start even earlier.'

Despite her tiredness, having to bake round the clock had been the best thing about these last few days. She'd had no time to dwell on *he whom she refused to remember*. Rafe certainly hadn't been into the bakery again, and now Alex was well enough to tend the roses, Gracie had stayed away from the villa.

'It' was definitely 'over', and that was just fine; she was choosing to think about something else. Anything else. Such as making pastries. Hundreds and hundreds of pastries. She'd been testing new products daily—to Francesca's delight. So the sleeplessness was worth it.

'I have news.' Francesca walked towards the counter.

'Good news?' Gracie looked up from wiping

down the cabinets. She needed as much distraction as possible.

'Catering news.' An awkward look crossed Francesca's face. 'A potential client wants to talk to you about an upcoming event.'

'When does she want to meet us?' Gracie paused and looked more intently at Francesca. Why was she looking guilty?

'This afternoon. He's requested you specifically. If we do well, it could open all kinds of doors given who's likely to be on the guest list.'

A sense of foreboding slithered down Gracie's spine. 'Who's *he*?'

'Rafael Vitale. The new owner of the Villa Rosetta. He wants us to cater his upcoming housewarming.'

Grace's heart thundered so loudly she put her hand to her chest to make sure her ribs could contain it. 'He's having a house-warming party?'

'A big one.' Francesca nodded. 'He said it would be better to communicate his needs in English with you.'

His *needs*? Four days and he'd suddenly realised he had *needs*?

A shadow crossed Francesca's face, dimming her excited glow. 'Are you sure you want to go? I can go with you if—'

'It's fine. No problem.' Gracie saw Francesca was torn about asking this of her. Rafael was in

the wrong for putting her friend in this position—
and he was going to hear about it. 'You need to be
here to get ready for tonight anyway.'

'You're sure? Fantastic. You're to meet him at
the villa at four o'clock. He said you already know
the security code to get in.' The interest in Francesca's gaze was barely veiled now.

'Yes, I know the code.' Gracie straightened and
shot her boss a smile and lied for the first time in
years. 'I'll handle him, no problem at all.'

At precisely four o'clock Gracie pressed the security code and the gate swung open. Once more she
walked up the stunning driveway. His too-flash,
too-fast car was parked in the driveway. Rafael
Vitale was standing by the shimmering pool. Tall,
dark and wet. He'd been swimming. Which meant
he was barely dressed. He was all muscles and hot-
ness. Gracie shot him a sharp look, but it simply
bounced off his brazenly smug smile. The guy had
done it deliberately.

Her pulse still thundered annoyingly loud in her
ears, hindering her chances of actually thinking.
But she was going to *try*. 'I hear you need more
pastries for your insatiable models?'

'That's right.' His smile widened.

'For a *house-warming* party?'

He spread his hands. 'I've been told this would
make a lovely home, rather than a luxury holiday

retreat, so I thought I'd see how it felt to live in it a little.'

'And that's your definition of living a little? Partying with pretty people?'

'Doesn't that match your definition?' he asked, brushing his wet hair back from his forehead and certifying his fallen angel's physique status. 'Of course not, you want to bury yourself in a sleepy little village with a bunch of octogenarians.'

Oh—he was going there? She drew in a careful breath because he was attacking *all* her senses. 'The village is hardly sleepy. It's full of tourists and easy-come, easy-go possibilities,' she muttered meaningfully. 'Lots and lots of tourists.'

His eyes narrowed. 'You think you've mastered that art now?'

She shrugged, but inside her pulse was thrumming unevenly. He had such an impact on her. Why couldn't the man put on clothes? 'Do you always turn up to business meetings in your swimsuit?'

'It's a hot day.'

But he'd known she was about to arrive and he'd dressed down deliberately. Whereas she'd dressed up. Wearing trousers had totally been the right call.

His smile was too bland given the sharpness of his eyes. 'I'm a wealthy potential client, isn't it your job to accommodate my eccentricities?'

She stared at him slack-jawed for a moment. 'And isn't it your job to behave like a decent human being and not use your…attributes to swing an advantage?'

'My attributes?' He echoed oh-so-innocently. 'I was hot.'

Yeah, he was always hot. She glared at him.

Eyes glinting, he slowly reached for a towel and wrapped it around his waist. 'Better?'

No, it wasn't any better. Somehow he looked even sexier. 'You don't play fair.'

At that satisfied expression on his face she mentally kicked herself. She needed to stop saying whatever was in her head when she was around him. Because it was always going to be inappropriate.

'I play to win.' He stepped closer. 'There are going to be a lot of people at the party,' he said temptingly. 'Lots of potential catering customers. Wealthy ones. Lots of good publicity with all those selfie-addict models and their social media circuses. You know they always love to snap beautiful food.'

'You're trying to bribe me.'

'You already knew I'm not a decent guy,' he said huskily. 'Why don't you come inside the villa to discuss arrangements? I can show you the facilities.'

'I believe I've already seen the facilities,' she

muttered, unable to resist playing on the double entendre sparking between them.

'Only briefly. I'm pretty sure I can give you a better understanding of what's available for you to use here.'

'For me to *use*…' She trailed off.

The wicked temptation in his eyes was too much. He knew exactly what effect he had on her. She could only hope she had even the smallest similar effect on him.

'It's too hot to stand outside,' he murmured coolly. 'You never know what madness might ensue if we stay out here too long.'

Well, that was certainly true. Awareness shot through her. It *was* what he wanted—she did indeed have the same effect on him. Her blood quickened but she wasn't going to make it that easy for him. Not this time.

She marched ahead, into the villa, pulling out her phone to take down details. 'How many guests are going to be at your housewarming?' She could be professional.

'Between fifty and seventy.'

'Quite the party.'

'Neighbours, work associates, friends…'

Lovers? She refused to ask. 'People you would like to impress?'

'People I'd like to feed,' he replied in a bored tone, following her into the kitchen. 'I take my responsibilities as a host very seriously. I'd like to meet the needs of all my guests.' He paused, leaning forward and putting his hands on the back of one of the chairs. 'I wouldn't want to leave anyone feeling hungry.'

'Hungry, huh?' Gracie gave up on the polite sham and tossed her phone onto the table, facing that blaze in his eyes. 'You used this as an excuse to get me here alone.'

'Yes.'

'Putting both me and my employer in a difficult position—you don't feel any remorse about that?'

'I like to get what I want.' He regarded her steadily. 'I generally do whatever it takes to get it.'

Playing dirty. Breaking the rules.

'You didn't think you could just *ask* for what you wanted?'

He stared at her for a second and then smiled reluctantly. 'I didn't want to risk you saying no again.'

She frowned.

'You were so eager to leave the other day, you didn't look back,' he elaborated.

'Wait. Do you think you *asked* me to stay?' She thought back to the other morning when she'd escaped as quickly as she could. She'd thought that was what he'd wanted—no sticky, awkward goodbye. But her swift departure had bothered him? She couldn't hold back a small smile. 'You told me you didn't want me to go. You never asked me to stay.'

His eyes narrowed ever so slightly.

'So you thought that once you'd got me here, you could convince me in person?' she asked.

'I thought it might help if I was mostly naked but that idea seems to have backfired.'

She noticed his grip on the back of the chair. His knuckles were white and his breathing, while even, was a little too quick. A trickle of power flowed through her veins. This was good, because he was too mesmerising and held too much of her attention.

'You've been away.' She made herself breathe.

'Yes. On business.'

She stepped closer. 'But you went to a party. In Paris.'

His eyes widened but he remained abnormally still. 'How do you know that?'

'There were pictures.'

'You searched for me on the Internet?' A teasing—smug—smile flashed on his perfect face. 'You set up an alert for me?'

'I didn't need to,' she informed him loftily. 'The village has been keeping an eye on what you've been up to and no less than three customers took the time to show me that picture of you with that model.'

'How kind. You must be so pleased with your

decision to live in a small town where everyone knows everything about everyone.'

'I'm not ashamed. I don't mind them knowing I spent time with you. I'll never regret what happened between us.' She kept her head high. Never was she going to be embarrassed about that.

'But?' he prompted softly.

'I'm not going to be your booty call. You can't just have me when you're home.'

'This isn't my home,' he said calmly. 'And that's not what I want either.'

She waited for him to explain.

He sighed. 'I was wrong about one night.'

'Oh?'

'Gracie.' He shook his head. 'You said you didn't play games. You said you'd be honest.'

And she had been. '*You* said you never wanted more than just sex.'

'And I'm still saying that. It's just that I want more than one night.' He drew in a breath. 'I don't want to resist you. You're all I can think about.'

It had been that good for him too? She bit her lip to stop herself smiling in a smug Rafe-like fashion. 'Yet you ran away.' She couldn't help teasing him softly. 'You left Italy. And it wasn't for work.'

'I thought it might help. It didn't.'

Goosebumps rippled over her skin. She was shockingly, pleasurably aware of his intensity.

'You left the country to escape me.' She took

another step closer. 'I don't know whether to be insulted or flattered.'

'Flattered,' he growled. 'And you missed me. You know you did. I saw it in your face the second you saw me again. I see it in the way you're looking at me now. Don't even try to lie.'

'You know I'm not going to,' she said simply, and stopped still. 'But we also both know this shouldn't happen again.'

'Why?'

'We want different things. You don't want a relationship.'

'Why does this have to be a relationship? You're inexperienced. Why not get some?'

'Experience?' she echoed innocently.

'There is so much you haven't done, Gracie.' The promise in his eyes was unmistakable. 'You wanted that wildness in amongst the precious. Why not just live in the moment?'

'Are you coming over all mindful?' She chuckled, her gaze dropping to his knuckles again. Heat stole over her as she registered just how tense he was.

'Don't make this into anything more than what it is,' he said with that roughness again. 'That is your inexperience showing.'

'But if it isn't anything all that, why did you have to leave?'

He closed his eyes briefly, huffing out a strangled laugh at the same time. 'Because it's strong. And in my experience, that's rare. I *want* you. I can't think of anything else.'

She knew that problem. The frustration. The desire that was inexorably drawing her closer now that he was back. And she saw the resistance within him. He was holding back—not touching her. Not letting his natural dominance be unleashed.

'Please, Gracie.' He was asking nicely and she was lost.

Slowly she walked closer. 'Who was the woman in Paris?'

'Isabella. I've known her since college. She's in a long-term relationship. We've never been lovers.'

Wow, so much information from one question. 'Did you want to be?'

He shook his head. 'She's not my type.'

A model who wasn't his type?

'I'm not a walking hormone, Gracie.' He glared at her. 'I don't want every woman I meet. Right now you're the *only* woman I want.'

She was hit by another rush of primal satisfaction. It served only to melt the last of her rational resistance. 'If we do this again, we're exclusive. I won't tolerate you sleeping with anyone else while you're doing that with me.'

'Doing "that"?' He half laughed. 'I'm insulted you'd think I would. I might've had a lot of lovers, but only ever one at a time. And when we're over, you'll be the first to know. For the record, I never use the next woman to end my relationship with the previous one. Don't you use another man against me either. Not even a seventy-year-old.'

She smiled. 'Alex is my friend and he cares about me. That's different.'

She walked the last few steps and knelt up on the chair right in front of him. His knuckles whitened.

'Gracie,' he groaned, and leaned closer. 'This isn't going to be only one night again. It's going to take more than that.'

'What happened to short time frames?'

'You want this,' he whispered, not answering her question. 'You want me.'

He was right. She'd been unable to think about anything else in these last few days. He'd completely dominated her thoughts. She couldn't even enjoy Alex's roses without thinking of him now.

'Absolutely,' she admitted. 'I adore you.'

'Adore?' He cocked his head like he wasn't sure what he was hearing.

'Don't panic.' She laughed weakly. 'It's just a phase. Like a crush. It'll pass and I'll get over it.'

He breathed out. 'You'll get over it more quickly if we let it run its course. The more we try to ignore it, the worse it's going to become.'

'I don't think it can get much worse,' she whispered.

He kissed her. His hands lifted. Somehow she

was on that big kitchen table and she was soaring with every sweep of his tongue.

'Why are you wearing trousers?' he muttered thickly.

'I didn't trust myself. I thought it might slow things down. I regret it now.'

He laughed and slid his hand beneath the waistband of her trousers. He drew in a deep breath. 'You're not ready for slow, Gracie.'

'No.' She arched breathlessly as he played her. 'I'm not.'

So not slow.

When she could think again, she reached up to touch him, but he grabbed her wrists and held them from him. 'Stay the night with me.' He smiled winningly. 'I'm asking nicely.'

'While holding me captive,' she teased.

He released her but stayed too close for her to think straight.

'You're saying no?' he asked.

She sat up and trailed her fingers down his chest and then grabbed his lean hips. 'Maybe we could do something more before I leave.'

He cupped her face gently. Too gently—it made her heart race unevenly.

'Why do you have to leave?' he asked. 'Life is precious, right? Why can't we be wicked and wild all night?'

She looked into his eyes and saw unspent passion blazing. Her bones trembled. He made her feel so good but this was more intense than she'd expected—which ought to have been impossible given what had happened between them the other day. She shouldn't stay, she felt a vulnerability curling within. 'I have an early start tomorrow.'

'Call in sick tomorrow,' he dared. 'Spend the day with me. All night. All day.'

He was joking but it was actually so tempting she got angry with herself—but turned it on him. 'You want me to ditch all my commitments? To drop everything else in my life to meet your sexual needs?'

'Not just *my* needs,' he pointed out, purposefully kissing her neck, apparently already confident of her surrender. 'You want this too.'

'I can't. I have to go,' she pleaded, but couldn't help tilting her head to let him have greater access. 'I can't let Francesca down. I have work. I can't just not show up.'

'Move in with me,' he said in a low voice. 'I'll work from here for a while and then we'll have all night, every night. At the weekends, you're mine. You do get weekends off, don't you?'

She was too busy trying to process his first words to be able to answer that last question. 'You want me to move in with you?'

He eased back and looked into her eyes. 'Briefly.'

She half laughed, her suddenly strung-out nerves getting the better of her. 'Well done on the clarification. Wouldn't want me getting the wrong idea.'

She *so* didn't want to get the wrong idea about this. But she couldn't believe what he'd just asked.

He grinned. 'I've been reliably informed honesty is the best policy.'

'Been talking to someone wise?' She desperately tried to maintain the teasing, but tension knotted her stomach. Staying with him—even briefly—was an alarmingly appealing idea and she instinctively shied from its strength.

'Someone with a smart mouth.'

He was joking. Surely. She tried to focus on all the practical reasons why she should say no. 'I start work very, very early.' And cycling from the villa would mean she'd have to wake even earlier.

'I'll drop you there. I'll have slept better with you beside me.'

Her innards melted at the thought of sleeping beside him night after night, of cuddling and curling close. Of being that intimate with him.

'Because it's still all about you,' she tried to joke, tried to stall, tried to steady her trembling slide towards his too-enticing invitation.

But there was a glint of outrageousness in his eyes and she just couldn't help warming like wax in his hands.

'Stay. I *promise* to make it worth your while.' He kissed her.

Oh, she didn't doubt it. What she doubted was her ability to leave again as 'easily' as she'd left the other day. Because that had been so difficult she'd had to run as quickly as she could. And she knew the more time she spent here, the harder it would become to leave again. It wasn't the villa and all its luxuries that posed the problem, but *him*. He was magnetic and his power over her only increased with exposure.

But she wanted him. She *ached* for his touch, his company. Her eyes closed as he kissed her again.

She should say no. She should just have the sex she'd said she wanted and escape. But her brain shorted out, refusing to process anything other than the delicious sensations he was pulling from every cell within her. The man knew how to make love. He knew how to make her want more. He knew how to make her say yes. Over and over again.

And that was terrible, because if he kept this up, she'd say yes to *everything*. And he didn't want everything, he only wanted this. Only now.

'You're incorrigible,' she admonished breathlessly.

'But I'm right.'

She quivered. It was more than his touch that tormented her, more than his sensuality and striking looks—it was his interest in all of her, his ability to fascinate her, his ability to make her laugh. If this were just sex, it would be easy. But it was all of him. She *liked* him, so much that she was in danger...but because he was all that, he was impossible to deny. She couldn't deny *herself*.

She sighed, her defences crumbling. 'Okay.'

'Okay? Just like that?' he teased.

Just like that? A helpless little laugh escaped.

'I'm hoping to get sick of you,' she admitted frankly, opening her eyes. 'Perhaps the more time I spend with you, the sooner that will happen.' She could only dream, right? 'And I can practise making some of the pastries in your oven if I stay.'

His mouth opened and then closed. Then opened again. 'You want to practise using my oven? *That's* why you want to stay?'

'It's one of the reasons.' She hid a smile. She'd got a tiny hit on him when he constantly overwhelmed her so completely. 'But I'm not cooking dinner for you,' she clarified, establishing a smidgeon of assertiveness. 'You're not getting a housekeeper as well as a bedmate.'

'If I wanted a housekeeper, I'd hire one.' He planted a kiss on her nose. 'I'm capable of cooking both for me and for you.'

'Is that so?'

'I enjoy eating so, yes, that's so,' he mocked, moving his kisses across her cheek. 'I'll cook for you, seeing as you're going to be my guest for a little while.'

A little while, right. His *guest*. Not his girlfriend or his live-in lover. She accepted this for what it was, a short-term fling and a risk she was going to make the most of. She'd keep it an indulgence for herself. She'd keep it calm.

'Perfect.' She ran her hand up his chest and pretended this wasn't all that perilous, pretended her heart wasn't pounding louder than a rocket launch.

But he stopped kissing her, pulling away to look into her eyes.

'What?' she queried breathlessly, poised right over the precipice.

'I hadn't expected you to agree so easily. I've been dreaming up other ways to convince you.'

'Oh.' She burned the last of her nerves in the bonfire of sensual anticipation and embraced the humour that bubbled so easily between them. 'Well, we can't let those ideas go to waste. I've changed my mind. Convince me to stay some more.'

'Too late,' he breathed, and pulled her to the edge of the table, a ferociously intense look in his eye. 'You're mine now.'

CHAPTER NINE

'WELL?' FRANCESCA LOOKED up from a mountain of flour the second Gracie walked into the café.

'Well, what?'

'How big is this party?' Francesca sounded amazed to have to explain. 'You didn't give me anywhere near enough information in your text message last night. Are you sure we can handle it? We can't even make enough pastries to last till closing each day.'

Gracie flushed and quickly turned to hang up her bag. She'd forgotten all about the party. 'Large but not impossible. It should be fairly straightforward as long as we start early. It's having enough stock here at the same time for those couple of days leading up to it that's the problem.'

'Well, I can always close early then if we have to,' Francesca mused. 'Often those clients prefer to get catering in from Milan or even further, I want to show them local is better.'

Which, now she thought about it, had been Rafe's point when they'd discussed it more late last night. He knew exactly how to play them. He knew how to win. Not that Gracie was complaining.

She worked swiftly. While several trays were baking she organised the small outside tables, putting one of Alex's roses in each of the small vases. Turning to go back inside, she was startled to see an elderly man staring at the table nearest him. She frowned in surprise—it was very early, there was almost no one else even moving in the village yet. And this old man hadn't shaved and looked dishevelled. He looked lost.

'I'm sorry, we're not open yet,' she said apologetically. But he didn't answer. He didn't stop staring at the rose she'd just put in the vase.

'Are you okay, sir? Can I help you?' she tried again.

Again, no reply. But his hands were trembling. He was clearly disoriented.

'Why don't you take a seat and I'll get you a drink?' Gracie said gently, lightly putting her hand on his shoulder to guide him. At her touch he looked at her and smiled.

'Thank you,' he said very formally with a crisp American accent.

'Something cool.' She smiled at him and gestured for him to take a seat. Even though it was early, the morning was warming quickly.

She quickly fetched a glass of the lemonade that Alex favoured and put a pastry on a plate for him as well. 'It's a beautiful rose, isn't it?' She set the refreshment in front of where he was sitting.

He nodded jerkily, lifting the glass to sip a small amount.

As she turned to go back inside, she saw another man striding along in the distance, looking down the narrow streets, concern carving the lines more deeply into his face.

She stepped forward to intercept him. 'Excuse me, are you looking—'

Gracie stopped and drew a steadying breath because she suddenly recognised this man. He was from that party the other night. Rafael had said he was his *nephew*. His much, much older nephew.

'Oh, there you are, Dad.' The man brushed past Gracie.

Dad? Gracie stared. If the elder man was the nephew's father, then he must be Rafael's half-brother. Her heart pounded. But she saw the confusion in the elder man's eyes. The lack of awareness, of recognition.

'I'm sorry he troubled you,' the nephew said briskly. 'He gets confused and wanders and I should have...'

He breathed out a harsh sigh and apologised again.

'It's okay.' Gracie smiled to put him at ease. 'It must be worrying.' She could see the stress he was under and she truly did understand.

'What do I owe you for the drink?'

'Nothing.' She smiled again. 'I'm just glad he's reunited with you.'

The man breathed out and relaxed fractionally.

Then he leaned forward to focus on the flower as well. 'Is that from the Villa Rosetta? They're famous for roses that colour.'

'Actually, no.' Gracie almost lost the strength in her legs. 'But it is one that's been grown by the villa's head gardener. He's very talented.'

'Right.' He nodded and helped his father to his feet. 'Thanks again.'

She watched them leave with a heaviness weighing down her chest. He'd reminded her of her own grandfather and that same confusion in his eyes. Aging wasn't easy.

'Is that man okay?' Francesca interrupted her thoughts as she went back into the small shop.

'Yes, he's fine now.' Gracie rolled her shoulders back, fretting over what had happened. She should tell Rafe. She just wasn't sure what she was going to say. 'Back to it.'

Hours later she looked out the window and saw Rafe pull in across the road. She grabbed the bags she'd prepared and dashed across to meet him.

'You've packed some clothes?' He grinned as he lifted them into the car for her.

'No, some ingredients.'

'Food?' He glanced again at the bags. 'You didn't pack any clothes?'

'I didn't think I'd need any.' She laughed and fastened her seatbelt.

'But you need ingredients?'

'I said I was going to try out your oven.'

'You can't be serious. You've been working all day and you have to be back at the bakery at stupid o'clock in the morning.' He drove them back to the villa.

'It's a stress release.' She giggled.

'I can help with that.' He sent her a look.

'You can, by telling me which of my pastries you prefer for your party. I need to get it organised.'

'And you're going to bake naked, right? Seeing as you didn't bring any clothes.'

'I'm not—' She broke off as music suddenly blasted from her phone. Her heart skidded—she'd saved that song for her mother. 'I'm sorry.' She glanced at Rafe. 'I need to get this.' She quickly swiped the screen. 'Mum, are you okay?'

'New brioche for breakfast.'

Gracie's heart sank at the code sentence her mother had always used for when they had to pack up quickly. 'You're moving again? Where to?' *Why?* There was no need for her to live such a nomadic existence any more.

'Portugal, I think,' her mother replied. 'I'm still deciding.'

'You could come and visit me,' Gracie invited softly.

'You know I can't return to Italy. Too many messy memories there. Look, I'll call again soon with my new details. I just wanted you to know so you didn't worry if you tried this number.'

'Okay,' Gracie answered, her heart sinking.

'Bye, darling. I love you.'

'Sure.' Gracie hung up and then scrolled through her phone, deleting her mother's contact details. Again.

'Your mother's moving?' Rafe quietly queried.

'Yes.' She tried to smile to cover that old ache. 'She never lasts more than a year in any one place.'

'But she's no longer in danger from the police because of hiding you, right?'

'Right,' Gracie answered. 'But she runs away from any kind of conflict. I mean, *any* kind. She just can't seem to settle.' And Gracie hated that. Her mother never stopped long enough to learn to trust anyone or any place. She never returned. She just kept on running. Never faced what it was that she feared most.

'How does she get by?'

'Oh, she's the best short-order cook you'll ever meet,' she said with a hiNt of pride. 'No one can cook meals in minutes like my mum.'

But Rafe didn't smile back, he looked concerned. 'You miss her.'

'Yeah.' Sadness bloomed again in the light of his perception. 'She was never *present*. She was always worried, always working to make the next buck. Not that she ever cooked for me,' she admitted ruefully. 'She was too tired when she got home.'

'Is that why you learned to cook?'

'I only ever baked—it was only about the pastry. I liked the science and taking the time to get it right. I spent hours in our little apartments, with all those crappy ovens, trying all different doughs.'

'Alone?'

She caught his inflection and smiled.

'But it was like therapy for you,' he said. 'That stress release.'

'Exactly. And you have a really nice kitchen, Rafe.' She got out of the car and headed into the villa with her bags to set up her space.

'You're not seriously about to make pastry now?' He followed her into the room.

'Actually, I am. Lots of little pastry cakes.' Because she needed time to clear her head and working soothed her. But then she glanced at him, because she wasn't alone now. 'Is that okay?'

'Of course. You know you're free to do what you want.' He lifted up the last of her heavy bags onto the bench. 'But do you mind if I watch?'

'You want to watch?' She frowned. 'I can't make small talk, Rafe, I need to concentrate.'

'I won't distract you.'

At that she finally smiled. Did the man not know he distracted her round the clock?

* * *

Ninety minutes later she presented five petite pastries on a plate for him—all gilded differently. She'd used glossy sabayon, smooth ganache, gold leaf, poached pear crisps...and so much more. She'd gone with miniature, intense works of art. True to his word, he hadn't distracted her—at least, not intentionally. He'd asked a few questions—to explain her methods—but otherwise he'd been quiet. And she'd relaxed into it. Now she saw the look on his face and pride licked. She was very good at what she did.

'You really like to present perfection, don't you? How am I supposed to choose?' He groaned and selected one while studying the others with gleaming eyes. 'You shouldn't be working for anyone. You should have your own bakery.'

She laughed. 'Thank you for that compliment.'

'I mean it.' He watched her, the curiosity in his eyes now professional as well as personal. 'I talked with a couple of local tourism leaders the other day. They said Bar Pasticceria Zullo has undergone a transformation in the last few months. It offers a far greater selection of sweets and is much more popular. Apparently the change coincides with your arrival.'

'Perhaps it coincides with the tourist season,' she muttered, her face heating. 'More people in town buying stuff.'

'You know that's not it.' He sent her a droll look. 'Why do you hide your light under a bushel?'

She wasn't. She was happy doing her thing with the people she'd found. 'Francesca has been really supportive of my ideas. I like working for her.'

'But why not work for yourself? You're doing all this work turning her business around for her. You should get the benefit.'

'Speaks the guy who likes to own everything in sight, even when he doesn't need it.' She laughed. She truly liked Francesca and she liked being part of the village. 'She's a good friend.'

'So you don't want your own bakery? You have an amazing product, you have good ideas. You know you have a head for marketing the business.' His eyes narrowed. 'Is it the start-up cost? You don't want to go into debt?'

'Are you about to make me an offer?' She smiled at the way he'd morphed into spot-the-deal CEO mode. 'Don't. My father offered to pay to set up my own bakery, and if I didn't take it from him, I'm not about to take it from you.'

'Why didn't you take it from him?' He looked up sharply, taking a moment to search her expression. 'There were strings?'

She sighed reluctantly, the guy was very perceptive. 'He wanted it to be in London.'

'And you didn't want to stay there?'

'I'd lived there with him for a while,' she said

quietly, refusing to think too deeply about that time. 'That way Mum didn't get punished more harshly when she came back into the country. She just had to pay a fine and do some community service and he left her alone.' She caught his frown. 'I was eighteen—no longer a child. It was my choice.'

'To protect your mother from repercussions?'

'Of course. She's my mother, Rafe. But he's my father and he and I both missed out. He wanted time with me and I wanted time with him.'

His expression tightened but he nodded slowly. 'How did it work out?'

'It was odd, initially,' she admitted. 'He'd remarried a few years back and I have a couple of half-brothers. I got on with them okay.' She sent him a quick sorry smile. 'They're cute.'

'But?'

She bit her lip. 'They're a family.'

'That you didn't feel part of?'

'It's complicated.' She shrugged it off and put on her smile. 'But I did my training when I was there. A really good culinary arts school, I did every extra course I could. Then I worked. Got great experience.'

'Evidently.' He nodded at the plate. 'So you kept busy.'

'Yes, and it was good. It was a great time. I was lucky that they all welcomed me.'

'Lucky,' he echoed.

'Yeah.' But she heard the suggestion of disbelief in his voice.

He studied her for a long moment and then took the plate of pastries from her and put it on the table. 'We have more in common than I'd thought.'

She laughed. 'No, we don't.'

'Sure we do.' He leaned in and tugged her towards him. 'Insatiable appetites, for a start.'

Rafe drummed his fingers on the steering wheel as he drove her to the *pasticceria*. The sky was barely beginning to lighten, but he felt sunny, warm and satisfied. Three days had passed since she'd first agreed to stay with him. Still not anywhere near enough time. Last night he'd woken her twice and then—to his supreme satisfaction— she'd woken him. Half an hour before her alarm, she'd roused him with her soft, hot mouth and her strong, silky-smooth thighs and that intoxicating, addictive passion.

He knew exactly how his day would play out and he couldn't be happier about it. He'd drop her at work, then return to the villa to get ahead of business so he could steal more time for himself later. In a few hours, when famished, he'd go back to the bakery, buy coffee and pastries and steal kisses.

While the café was closed for the early afternoon he'd walk with her while she checked on Alex. She always saved the old guy a pastry, even though they'd sold out to the paying customers. Alex waited in his chair in the shade, a carafe of his favourite lemonade on the table and two glasses. In the last couple of days there'd been three glasses waiting.

Rafael talked to him about the roses and the history of the villa, but he'd not asked Alex if he'd met his father when he'd stayed there all those years ago. Some things were better off untouched. But he enjoyed the banter between Alex and Gracie. She'd tell him stories of the tourists and who from the village had been into the café, while he asked questions and made acerbic comments. He saw the appreciation in the old guy's eyes and he was almost not jealous.

After visiting Alex, he'd take her to the villa for a lazy swim and sex. She didn't have to work the late shift tonight and he was looking forward to having the entire evening with her. But when he pulled up at the *pasticceria*, Gracie got out of the car and sent him a sparkling smile through the open window. 'I can't stay with you tonight. I'm having dinner with Alex, so I'll sleep at home.'

At home? He blinked at her. Did she mean her apartment?

'You have lunch with him every day.' Stupidly strong disappointment forced his immediate argument. The suggestion sucked the sweet wind right out of his sails. She hadn't even left and he'd already been looking forward to her returning. Frankly, he didn't want her to leave at all and that fact bothered him too. In an instant he was bothered by everything—unreasonably irritated at the thought of not seeing her for an entire day.

'Are you jealous?' She smiled at him.

'Yes.' She was going to be smiling at Alex tonight. While the villa was going to be quiet and his bed cold.

'You'll get over it. It'll pass.' She smiled at him triumphantly and turned to walk away.

Rafe watched her go. She'd waited until she'd got out of the car before telling him. Why? Because she'd known he'd have tried to convince her otherwise and they both knew he would have succeeded. That soothed his irritation somewhat, but he wouldn't go back to the bakery for coffee later. He couldn't see her in public when it was going to be an entire day and night until he was *alone* with her again. But by evening he was bored out of his brain. He didn't want to rattle around the villa alone without her.

He went for a drive, telling himself he'd go to the next village along from Bellezzo. Except Pasticceria Zullo had the best food and the best atmosphere. He couldn't resist walking past just to see how busy it was. He approached it by the side

alley. The rear entrance was open to let the heat of
the kitchen out. He paused some distance away because he could see a woman working over a mountain of dough. Not just any woman. Her face was
flushed as she kneaded. He could see the tiredness in her stance but worse was the droop of her
mouth. He knew Gracie—he knew her smile. And
right now he knew she was sad. But he was furious. She was *working*?

He watched from the alley a while longer. Why
had she lied to him? He'd have understood if she'd
needed to work. He'd happily have waited and
given her a lift back home to his place. It seemed
so unusual for her to lie, especially when she'd
said she never wanted to do that any more. He
walked to the front of the bar and came to another halt.

Alex was sitting at one of the tables outside,
a younger man and woman sitting on either side
of him, and there was no spare chair waiting for
Gracie.

Rafe frowned and walked straight over. 'I
thought Gracie was having dinner with you tonight, Alex.'

Alex looked up. 'Rafael—'

But Rafe was watching the others and caught
the awkward look between what was clearly Alex's son and his wife.

'She decided to let us have time, just us family,' the son interjected before Alex could say anything more.

Just us family.

And they didn't consider Gracie family? When she had been the one looking after Alex when he'd been ill? When she'd been the one checking on him every single day? When she was the one who wanted nothing more than a family of her own?

The irritation that had been smouldering within him all day sparked to a full flame of anger.

'She said she was tired,' Alex said unhappily. 'I asked her to stay.'

'She doesn't want to stay with you all the time, Father,' Alex's son said. 'Most young women don't want to hang around old men.'

It sounded like he was the one who didn't want *her* around. Rafe glanced at the man, fury slicing through him. 'Why? You think she's targeting your father like some gold-digger hunting a sugar daddy?' He grimaced at the shock that flashed on the man's face. Damn it, not everyone had the history he did. He drew a breath and backtracked with truth. 'Gracie *cares* for Alex. She does everything she can for him every day. Just as she does for *anyone* who asks her. She likes to help people.'

And thanks to their thoughtlessness, she was now alone. *Again.*

'Rafe?'

He froze. Gracie was standing behind him, wearing a flour-sprinkled apron, and she was as pale as that flour, save for two red spots blooming high on her cheekbones.

'What are you doing here?' she whispered, glancing around at all the other people who'd just heard what he'd said.

He didn't care about the other customers, he cared about her.

And that realisation made him flounder. 'You...' He swallowed, then swiftly stepped forward. 'You said you were having dinner with Alex.'

'That was the original plan, but his family turned up for a surprise visit,' she answered, her soft eyes full of emotion.

And she'd been dispatched. 'So now you're working *again*?' he asked.

A chair scraped on the cobbles as Alex stood. 'Gracie—'

'Please, sit down, Alex, and enjoy your meal with your family.' She leaned past Rafe to offer the old man a smile, her flush steadily growing. 'It's fine. Rafe just got confused about...things. I'll take him away.'

Because he was misbehaving? He followed her into the *pasticceria*. She picked up a large slice of pizza and offered it to him, her eyes not quite meeting his. 'Would you like some?'

Oh, no, she wasn't going to take care of *him* now.

'What about you? Have you eaten?' he demanded.

Surprise flashed on her face, then she averted her eyes again.

Of course she hadn't eaten. He stalked behind the counter and took the pizza from her. He reached for an empty box from behind her, put that piece in and then added more. 'No doubt it's hours since you last ate properly.'

'You go, Gracie.' Francesca emerged from the kitchen, a subdued look on her face when she glanced at Rafe. 'I can handle the café.'

'You're sure?' Gracie double-checked.

Of course she checked. Rafe felt even more irritated. Couldn't Gracie put *herself* first for once, instead of trying to be all things to everyone?

He walked her to his car. She got into the passenger seat and he handed her the pizza box. He took a couple of deep breaths as he walked around the car to the driver's door. He shouldn't be this worked up, but he couldn't shake it off. This protectiveness? Just instinct, right? Normal levels of concern for a nice person.

'I'm sorry for interrupting Alex's dinner,' he said, starting the engine to get out of the village as fast as possible.

She slowly swivelled to face him, the pizza balanced precariously on her knee. 'You thought they'd been rude to me?'

He sighed. 'You said you were going to dinner with Alex. I saw you in the kitchen from the alley. You were alone and you looked sad and then they were there all having a nice dinner without you and, yes, I thought they'd been rude to you.' He clenched the steering wheel as he thought about it. He sounded like some stalker. Hell, he *was* some stalker. But he'd been worried. And annoyed. And she still looked sad, even if she was trying not to.

Though why he felt *this* mad about it, why he'd chastised those strangers, why he'd insisted on ensuring she was okay... He just felt an incredibly strong need to be with her. To take care of her.

'I wanted them to have some space. It was my choice,' she replied with a determined smile. 'They just wanted to spend some time together as a family. It's nice.'

But he'd seen her loneliness, he heard it in her voice now—because she didn't have the kind of family she wanted. She'd treated Alex as family, and for his son to have rejected her?

'It would also have been nice for you to spend time with them,' he pointed out with more gentleness than he was feeling. 'You care for him like family.'

Rafe had been isolated and treated with suspicion, been looked down on, and it had hurt, and Gracie didn't deserve that from those people. She had a kind, generous heart. Fury rose all over again at the thought of them dismissing her. He glanced at her but his rage was derailed because her expression had crumpled. He instinctively slowed the car. 'Hey—'

'Thank you for standing up for me,' she muttered quietly. '*That* was nice.'

His chest tightened and he swallowed, not quite sure how to respond.

But then she smiled. 'Your first instinct is to think the worst of everyone, isn't it? You don't trust anyone.'

His pulse thundered even more. 'You heard that bit? Damn.' He shook his head and dragged up a rueful smile. 'I'm sorry.'

'No, it's okay.' Her expression sweetened and she put her hand on his. 'Alex would never think that I was after something from him. I don't think his son would either.' She looked at him with those tender eyes. 'What made your mind even *go* there?'

'My mother,' he said bitterly, pulling in to park at the villa. 'That's who she was, right? The gold-digging slut who seduced septuagenarians for their megabucks.' He looked at her. 'All my life people have thrown that rubbish at me. I don't want them saying anything like that to you.'

'Rafe, they wouldn't. They didn't. And even if they had…you know I can take care of myself.'

'Can you?' Warm amusement muted his earlier

annoyance. He released his seatbelt and turned to her. 'Gracie, you're like a marshmallow melting into a mug of chocolate to sweeten it up. You like to make a difference. You like to be needed.' And right now her friend Alex didn't need her. But Rafe did. He wanted to think she might need him too. Just for the moment.

She lifted a shoulder in a little shrug. 'And what's wrong with liking to be needed?'

'Because you do it at the expense of your *own* needs. Of your own welfare.'

'No, I—'

'Stop, Gracie.' He turned his hand and grasped her fingers before she could tug them away. 'Enough of the pretence. Your whole "life's perfect" performance. You were lonely tonight. And you were sad. You're still sad, I can see it in your eyes. Be as honest as you always say you are.'

'Okay, I was sad,' she admitted quietly. 'I saw them and they were so natural and happy together and I felt down and I excused myself from the dinner because…'

'You didn't want happy families in your face.'

She shrank a little in her seat. 'It sounds so bitter and jealous.'

'No, you're not either of those things, but after what you've been through I wouldn't blame you if you were.' He put his arm around her. 'So you opted to work?'

'Francesca was run off her feet, trying to get prepared because one of the crew was late...'

'And it's your stress release—you work out your worry, right?'

She nodded.

'You're too generous,' he added quietly. 'You let people take advantage of you.'

'Is that what you're doing?' she teased.

He released her with a sigh and got out of the car. 'You know I am.'

'You don't think I'm getting anything out of this?' She laughed lightly as she joined him. 'I'm getting all the experience I've missed out on in all these years.'

'Because you're so ancient?' He tried to tease her back. But there was still an ache in his chest.

He should have been relieved at her assertion that this was a win-win transaction between them but it only compounded his tension. Was this only about sex? As if he were her intimate tutor? He didn't quite know what he was—what *this* was—but it was more than that. But even as he wanted that, he rejected it. That it was so easy to spend time with her made him *uneasy*. Yet at the same time he ached for that time to be endless.

He understood that she'd wanted companionship tonight, but she'd sought it from her old friend, not him. And when her friend had been busy, she'd opted to work. Was that because she didn't regard *him* as a friend? His discomfort bubbled back. He could be one of those—better than Alex, or Francesca. Better than anyone.

His pulse thrummed. He had no freaking idea how to be a *friend*. He'd never trusted anyone to get close, not after the nightmare of his half-brother and then boarding school. He'd always been fighting—for respect, for success. He'd long ago given up needing or wanting real acceptance. The irony was now he had all that 'success', people craved his company. But other than in hedonistic pursuits, he had no real idea how to relate. The realisation he was incompetent at something curdled his stomach acid. He snagged her arm and led her towards the boat shed instead of the home.

'We're not going inside?' Gracie asked, still holding the damn pizza box.

'There's a lot of light left in the day. Let's just enjoy the sun and eat pizza.'

He needed the fresh air. He probably needed the pizza. He definitely needed to see her smile. He unlocked the boat shed and gestured for her to go in, snagging the pizza box from her as she went past.

'This is amazing.' She stared at the interior of the boat shed. 'There's *stained glass* in here, Rafe. Look at the detail in this window.'

Admittedly it was more like a museum than a workshop space.

'I've not been in here much,' he confessed. 'But

this is the real treasure.' He pointed to the beautiful wooden boat. 'She's vintage, even older than your bike, I believe. I'm sure you'll appreciate her.'

'You're right.' She laughed lightly and bent down to inspect the mahogany hull. '*Rosabella.* She's beautiful. Look at the craftsmanship.'

'Shall we take her out?' Two bites of that pizza and watching Gracie run her hand over the hull of the boat and Rafe was feeling better about everything.

'Do you know how to drive her?' she asked as he handed her some pizza and untied the mooring rope.

'I'm sure I can figure it out.'

'Move over,' she said confidently.

He watched her study the engine instruments with undisguised interest. A second later she was checking the fuel. She knew what she was doing. And he was happy to let her take charge. He'd seen her tinkering with her bike, with the ovens; she knew machinery. And ten minutes later they were cruising across the water.

'Okay, so when did you learn to drive a boat?' he asked, happily finishing the last piece of pizza.

'For a while we lived in the South of France and I lived next to a large family. They had a family fishing business and were always fixing their gear themselves. I watched. Then I helped.'

From the warmth in her voice he knew she'd enjoyed that time. 'Did you ever go back to see them? Later, when you'd come out of hiding?'

Her expression froze and she busied herself with fiddling with one of the chrome gauges.

'Gracie?'

'People move on,' she said with a determined smile that he just knew hid heartache. 'I was only there about ten months, and when you go, people get on with their lives without you.'

'So you went back?'

She sighed and sent him a look. 'I did. Years later. And sure enough they were busy with their own families, their own friends—people they'd known all their lives. When you're only around for a short period, you're easy to forget.' She shrugged as if it all made perfect sense.

And it had only been short periods that she'd stayed in each place. So she'd felt forgotten? Unwanted? *Unloved.* Now he began to understand her current resistance to a nomadic existence. And why she worked so hard to fit into Bellezzo and be needed.

His stomach knotted. 'I can't imagine anyone forgetting you.'

She chuckled again. 'That's just another example of your feeble imagination.'

He laughed, as she'd intended, but he kept thinking as well. She'd been so lonely. That was why she wanted to put down roots, why she warmed to the merest touch of friendliness, why she worked so hard to make herself indispensable. And she knew that he saw that need in her—to be wanted. Her expression tightened.

'You leapt to my defence so swiftly tonight,' she said quietly. 'Is that what you did for your mother?'

He knew she was asking this to deflect his thoughts from her. Doubtless she thought he'd distract her with desire the way he usually did. But not this time. Somehow it seemed important that she *understand*. He wanted her to know everything about him, the way he wanted to know everything about her.

'I wish I could have,' he replied. 'But I hardly had the chance. She died when I was twelve.'

'Only a few years after your father?' She frowned. 'But she was so much younger—what happened?'

'You know my father was over seventy when I was born. My half-siblings were not impressed. They successfully stopped him from marrying her. She refused, because she knew they hated her. They tried to have him declared mentally incompetent, and when that failed, they just waited for the inevitable. The moment Roland died the accusations flew openly—was I even his son? Roland had vetoed any DNA testing, saying it was insulting to my mum. For his will, it was essential.' The public shame and humiliation of the procedure still swept over him when he thought of it.

'And you were his son.'

'Yes. Of course. It seems impossible for anyone else to believe, but they did love each other.'

'So the test silenced the wider family?'

If only. 'Suddenly I was an heir and a future Butler-Ross. Apparently that meant I needed "protecting".'

'From?'

'My mother.'

'What?' She stared at him, her eyes widening in horror. *'No.'*

'Money brings so much power, Gracie,' he said grimly. 'They told her I'd be better off with the education, the connections that the family could offer. That she had nothing to offer me that could compete with all they had.'

'But—'

'I know.' He held up his hand and smiled at her. 'And she argued exactly that—she was my mother and she loved me. But then they threatened— courts, custody, you know the drill precisely. They pressured her, she believed she couldn't compete. She didn't have the money or the support. So she agreed to their terms. They paid her off, but she still thought we'd see each other.'

'You didn't?'

'I was the illegitimate secret sent to a boarding

school on the other side of the country to be smartened up. They used the promise of a visit from her as a reward for good behaviour. If I did well, I'd get to see her. And if I was really good, maybe I could even come to the villa they loved to holiday at in Italy. The one our father had always stayed at for a few months each year...'

'Oh, Rafe. Did they never let you?' She glanced back across the water to the beautiful villa—it had been that symbol of happiness, so out of reach for so long.

'No. And in those years my mother was very unhappy, and she became unwell.'

She looked up at him with those emotion-laden eyes.

'Addiction,' he said softly.

'I'm so sorry.'

Numbing her nightmare, filling the gaping holes inside with temporary plugs.

'She was beautiful, you know. That's how I like to remember her.' Not from the photographs his horrendous half-brother Leonard had so maliciously shown him. 'Valentina Vitale—not her real name obviously.' He smiled in reminiscence. 'She made it up to sound more Italian. She actually *was* Italian, on her mother's side, but Valentina Vitale sounded more glamorous. As does Rafael Vitale.' He sent her an ironic glance. 'I was her angel baby after all.' She had loved him. She and the old man had doted on him when he'd been small. He had few memories of that time, but the ones he had were good.

'And so you've kept your name, not your father's.'

'They wouldn't let me have it until after he died and then they tried to force me to change it. But I am who I am and I was hers,' he said roughly. 'My name was what *she* gave me. I'll never hide or change that.' He would never let her be forgotten.

'I changed my name so many times and I hated it.'

'Yeah.' Identity mattered. He put his hand over hers. 'Don't you hate your parents for what happened?'

She looked over the water. 'They both thought they wanted the best for me, but they were so busy fighting they forgot what I really needed. Just a home, Rafe. That's all. Security. Instead, I became the bone between them. And I still can't win. I still can't choose. So I visit them each at least once each year and otherwise just stay here. But I don't hate them, I get it. They love me in their way.'

'You're determined to be positive about it?'

'Well, why would I want to be miserable?' She turned back to the water.

'Because what happened *was* miserable,' he said simply. 'Because you were isolated and without roots for years and it's okay to feel rotten about it sometimes. And, yes, you've chosen your new home town and it's lovely but not everything is perfect all of the time. Like tonight. You felt lonely and to bury it you went back to work.'

'Well, wasn't that better than sitting alone and moping?'

But she hadn't needed to sit home alone. She could have come to *him*. And it still hurt that she hadn't.

Beneath his, her hand tightened on the wheel. 'Let's see how fast we can get this girl to go, shall we?'

She was the one distracting and deflecting this time, but he decided to let her. Because he was exposed too. He never had told anyone else what had happened to his mother.

'You're a secret speed freak,' he said with a smile.

'Not *so* secret,' she purred, and pushed the boat's motor until the wind whipped her hair from its braid and her own smile was wide and her eyes sparkled.

'You want a turn?' She turned to him after a while.

'I wasn't sure you'd ever be able to give up the steering wheel.'

'Well, it is a wrench,' she acknowledged archly, lifting her hand from the wheel. 'Promise me you won't crash it.'

'Have a little faith.'

'But you're a novice, right?'

Not completely, but he was enjoying the joke. 'That doesn't mean I'm going to be useless,' he answered in mock outrage. 'You weren't useless when you were a novice.'

'Because I'm a quick learner.' She smiled smugly.

'And you don't think I can be?'

'You don't need to be. You already have everything just the way you want it. Your game is all figured out.'

He didn't reply. Only a few days ago he'd have agreed with her completely. But his confidence in his choices now was oddly diminished. The only thing he was sure about at the moment was that he wanted to take her back to the villa. He steadily chugged the boat across the water. After a few minutes he glanced behind him to where she'd curled up on the plush seat and caught her covering a yawn.

'We're nearly there,' he said.

'It's truly spectacular,' she said with sleepy softness. 'Do you pinch yourself when you remember it's yours?'

He smiled.

'Oh, no, that's right, you own so *many* amazing properties—not homes—you must get blasé about them all.'

He didn't stop to think about them much. They were places to sleep. But there was something about this one—the classical beauty of it perhaps, with that perfect symmetrical architecture.

No. It wasn't the architecture. Something else tugged deep in his chest when he looked at that villa and it wasn't the childhood memories of his father's stories—those were old feel-good fantasies. This was present-day laughter, warmth, life. This was all Gracie.

He cruised into the narrow channel that led to the boat shed. He turned the engine off and secured the boat in her berth. Then he turned to Gracie. She lay curled in a ball, her head resting on the cushion, her eyes closed. His skin chilled. Only now did he note the shadows beneath her eyes, the pallor of her skin and that droop to her mouth again—it wasn't just sadness.

'You're exhausted,' he growled, and scooped her into his arms, suppressing that caveman satisfaction that flickered every time he held her like this.

'What?' Her eyes flashed open and she turned on a smile. 'I'm fine.'

'You're not fine.' He rolled his eyes. 'Don't be out here just to please me, Gracie. That's not how things are for us.'

'I'm having a nice time.' She even put her arms around his neck as if to prove it.

And okay he knew it was true, but it wasn't *all* the truth. 'But you're also really tired. Put your own needs first for once, Gracie.' He frowned. 'Did you lie to me about the dinner with Alex? Did you want to stay home alone just to get a good night's sleep?'

'No, I wouldn't lie about that.' She jerked her head in a tiny motion. But then a flicker of guilt flashed across her beautiful features. 'But, okay, you're right. I was going to have an early dinner with Alex and I was sad when I saw him with his son. And, yes, the late nights with you are taking a toll. I want to stay so much,' she added hurriedly in that babbling way she had when she was anxious. 'But I'm usually a lark and go to bed super early and I was going to have an early night to-night.'

But she could have had an early night here with him—all she'd had to do was talk to him and *say* how she was feeling. But she hadn't. Why? Was she worried about his reaction? Did she think she had to please him all the time?

Guilt struck him like a stone thrown from be-hind. He was a selfish jerk. He hadn't thought at all about the impact their hedonism might have on her—especially when she worked on her feet all day. He carried her up to his bed. She mut-tered something unintelligible as he lowered her to the mattress, but he suppressed the desire to waken her fully and please her the way he ached to. She needed rest more than she needed passion. He quickly stripped and got into bed to cuddle her gently. In moments she was fast asleep. His very own Sleeping Beauty once again.

He chose not to wake her during the night, despite the fact he couldn't sleep for the burning desire low in his belly. Instead, he watched her sleeping, curved against him, her skin creamy and pale in the moonlight, a light flush on those pretty cheeks from the warm evening. She worked so hard and was so loyal, doing nice things for everyone in her life. She deserved something nice in return.

The answer arrived in the smallest of hours. What she needed was a few days off. An actual, real holiday. She was always doing everything for everyone else. Perhaps that was one thing he could give to her.

CHAPTER TEN

GRACIE DRAGGED HER comb through her hair, determined to take each day with delight. She was living 'in the moment', which basically meant point-blank refusing to think beyond bedtime. Truth be told, she was struggling to think of anything *but* bedtime. Especially when she'd fallen asleep last night and missed out entirely on the intimacy she enjoyed so much with him—even more because she'd felt closer to him than ever after what he'd told her.

And what he'd pointed out. He'd seen through her—to the loneliness she'd felt and that lingering hurt from years before. But what was more unsettling was that he'd admitted his own.

But then she'd slept right through till the alarm he'd set and she'd had to scramble for the shower because otherwise she was going to be late for work.

'I have to go to Paris for a few days. Meetings.' Rafael walked into the bathroom and wrapped his arms around her, stopping her from fixing her bed hair.

'Nice.' Gracie nodded, not paying all that much attention to what he was saying—how could she, when he was bare-chested and she was quivering with unquenched desire for him? All she wanted to do was embrace him and hold him close for ever.

'Come with me.'

She sharpened her focus on his words rather than his looks. 'You mean to Paris?'

'Yes, to Paris.' He mocked her breathiness.

She leaned back to look into his face and see his expression. This time she made herself ignore all the bronzed skin and sharply defined muscles in front of her. She swallowed.

The whisper of uncertainty she'd been feeling all morning thickened into a fog. This was only supposed to be her indulgence—a few days, that was all. He could not possibly be offering her this in the way she so desperately wanted him to mean.

She'd not told him quite everything last night. Her dinner arrangement with Alex had been a little self-administered test for herself. To see if she could have a night away from Rafe, to ensure she still had control of this. Of her heart. And when he'd shown up? She had been stupidly happy to see him. When he'd stood up to Alex's son, even though he'd jumped to the wrong conclusion, her heart had stopped altogether. So touched. He'd seen through her—to her pain, to her tiredness—and that hour with him on the boat had been one of the best hours of her life…so she was in such trouble. A romantic weekend in Paris was only going to further blur the boundaries for her. Because she'd love it. She'd love it far too much.

'I have a job.' She cleared her throat. 'A job I

usually work double shifts at. Not to mention your party is next week, or have you forgotten that? And I have other things to do in Bellezzo.'

'There are other things to do in Paris too. You can go to all the pastry shops. You could consider it a work trip if you must.' He pulled her closer. 'It's only for a few days. We could dine at a different restaurant every night, we could walk along the river, we could even dance... When was the last time you had a holiday?'

It was so tempting that she couldn't quite bring herself to say no right away. But somehow he already knew.

'You're not going to say yes,' he said, a frown growing on his face.

'I can't say I'm not tempted.' She couldn't lie. She was unbearably tempted, but that was exactly why she couldn't say yes. She put her palm on his chest, feeling the steady beat of his heart. 'But I don't want to tear around the place following...not just you, not anyone.' She hoped he'd understand this, he *had* to understand. 'I've done that most of my life. I want just the one place. I want a home.'

'I'm not asking you to leave your job and never return.' He couldn't quite keep the sarcasm out of his reply. 'It's only for a few days.'

'At the height of the tourist season here. People are counting on me. I'm not going to let Francesca down.'

Francesca had been the next to welcome her after Alex. She'd given her a job, she'd let her experiment. Gracie owed her.

'We can find another designer dress and hit the Paris Opera,' Rafe wheedled with a wink. 'I'm sure I can find fireworks or fountains to entertain you with.'

'That was fun as a one-off...'

'You know you can't resist.'

And there was the problem. She needed to know she *could* resist. She felt vulnerable, like she was teetering on the brink of a very big black hole.

'I can if you're not going to be here.' She smiled.

But he didn't smile back. 'You need this trip.'

'Do I?' She felt suddenly edgy.

She couldn't let him tempt her. Then she'd have given way on everything—to sleeping with him, to staying with him, to going away with him. After her parents' war with her as collateral, she'd sworn not to lose control of her life again, not to allow someone else to make all the decisions—but Rafe threatened more than that. He threatened her heart.

'I thought you were all about being brave and honest and adventurous,' he said. 'You told me life was precious. And you wanted some wildness.'

'And Paris is going to be wild?' She tried to tease but it sounded petulant and bitter. Right now she *was* bitter. This wasn't what they'd agreed. It wasn't fair of him to change the rules now when she knew he didn't want anything more than this. For him it was just a fun affair.

'With me, sure.'

She shook her head. 'I can't go with you.'

'You want to spend the rest of your life hiding in this sleepy village?' His frustration became audible.

'I'm not hiding. I'm *happy*.'

'Are you? So happy that you fall into bed with the first man who shows you some interest?'

Shocked, she stared at him. That hit *hurt*. 'Do you really think you were the first man to show interest in me? That you were the only chance I've ever had?' She pulled herself up haughtily. 'Don't go thinking you did me a favour. *I* picked *you*.'

'So pick me again,' he dared coolly. 'Come to Paris.'

'I don't want to go to Paris. I don't want to go anywhere.'

'You just want to fritter away your life doing nothing here? You're letting your skills go to waste. You should have your *own* bakery, not work all hours building a business for someone else. And you're never going to meet the man of your dreams while living with a bunch of oldies in this sleepy little village.'

His words slapped because the cruel irony was she'd done exactly that. She'd met *him*. But she was nothing more than *his* summer holiday fling—merely a way to pass the time while he decided what to do with his latest *possession*. In fact, wasn't she just another of those?

'Perhaps I only want short affairs with tourists passing through,' she sniped.

'Gracie, please.' He looked wild, then visibly tried to recover his temper. 'You need a rest. You know you do.'

'Yes. Maybe now is a good time for us to have a rest from each other,' she said quietly, ignoring the tightening in her lungs. She needed to know she *could* have that break from him.

He glared at her. 'I offer you the chance to go to Paris and you're angry with me.'

'And you're angry with me,' she replied tightly, trying to hold on to her emotions. 'It seems we've disappointed each other.'

'I just wanted to do something nice. Us. To-gether.' He growled. 'Something that isn't...' He gestured in futility.

But there was no 'us', and they weren't going to be *together*. Not for long. He'd made that perfectly clear from the start and she knew he wasn't going to change his mind. He was messing this up and she couldn't let him. She felt more at risk than she'd been even in those years abroad with her mother, and it scared her.

'What is it you don't like about Paris?' he prodded with a forced smile. 'The food?'

'Of course not,' she said. Sadness rose within her—the sadness she'd always suppressed. 'For years my life was uprooted on a whim. Mum allowed me one bag and we had to steal away in the middle of the night countless times. I had to leave all the things I'd tried so hard to build. I don't want to just jump to someone's orders like that ever again.

'I know you didn't mean it that way, I know it's only a few days…but I'm still… I'm still mastering the art of navigating my own ship. I don't want to jump just because you've asked me to.' She looked into his face, willing him to understand. 'And that dress, for that party at the *palazzo*—that was a one-off. I'm not Cinderella, you're not my fairy godmother or my Prince Charming, I don't want to take things from you in that way. This thing between us isn't like that.'

'This thing?'

'Yes. This affair.'

'It's an affair?'

She flushed and anger gleamed in her eyes. 'I don't know what to call it. I just don't want it to become any more complicated.'

Somehow he was irritated again as well. 'So I'm not to come back with an emerald bracelet or diamond necklace for you, my current lover?'

'Of course not.' She was appalled at the thought. Was that what he did for other women he'd slept with? She hated that idea—she didn't know that side of him at all. And she didn't want to.

'You don't like gifts?'

'No.'

'So, no gifts, no travel. What *do* you like?'

She liked *him*. Her heart pounded as she answered. 'Control.'

'Really?' His eyebrows arched. 'You don't want anything else from me apart from this?' He drew her closer.

'I really don't.' She sucked in a breath. 'I only want what we agreed. Only you. Only now.'

For some reason Rafe was even angrier when he really should have been relieved. She was holding fast to their initial agreement. But once again, when she delivered what he'd thought he wanted from her, he found he wanted the exact opposite.

'So have me, then,' he challenged her bluntly.

He didn't want to talk any more, didn't want to question. He wanted to make her pay. He'd tease and torment her so she'd be unable to forget him for these few days he'd be away. He wanted her to *regret* this rejection.

'I don't want to fight,' he muttered, stripping her out of her underwear.

But in a way he wanted exactly that. Here and now.

He hoisted her into his arms, holding her so he could kiss her exactly where and how he knew she liked it the most. Making her moan, making her shake with urgency and need until she was twisting beneath him. But he wouldn't give her what she wanted. Not yet. Not when she frustrated him so completely. He was irritated with himself for wanting her so badly, as much as he was irritated with her refusal to go away with him. He couldn't hold back the emotion he felt from her rejection and he demanded recompense. He wanted to make her want him more than she'd ever wanted anything in her life. Hell, he was turning into a complete egotist.

He'd leave for Paris immediately—get his meetings concluded quickly so he could come back and burn this out entirely and then he'd go back home to Manhattan. He'd been here too long already anyway. That'd leave her free to find whatever it was her heart wanted. Because he knew it wouldn't be him for much longer. But in kissing her, in touching her, it was his own control that slipped.

'Rafe. *Rafe*,' she begged him. 'Please, please.'

She was so responsive, so welcoming, so damn hot. And so deliciously quick. In the end he couldn't resist his own driving need to get close to her again. To make peace. He wanted her too much. His plan to make her pay was shredded as emotion claimed control of his mind and body. He didn't want her to be angry, but happy. Content. Glowing. To welcome him, to move with him. Together. In the end, the only thing he could gift her in this moment was himself.

CHAPTER ELEVEN

GRACIE RUBBED HER bare wrist again, annoyed at the emptiness. In her dishevelled panic to get to work on time after that crazy, passionate moment, she'd left her watch in his bedroom. Not wearing it irritated her completely.

Okay, it wasn't just the missing watch irritating her. She missed him more than she'd have believed possible. Not only the intense sensuality they shared but the shared amusement. She thought of him, dreamed of him…wanted to *talk* to him. She missed his conversation, his insights, his astuteness.

Yeah, she was in such trouble. That last time, the morning when he'd asked her to go to Paris with him, had been unbearably intense. If that was make-up sex, then maybe she wanted to fight with him more often. Truthfully, she'd been afraid of fighting. She hadn't wanted to lose him before their time was up. But she hadn't.

Though she hadn't realised he was going away so soon either. He'd left that morning. And sure, he'd called her a couple of times—teasing that he wasn't going to any parties for fear of pictures of him being snapped and posted on social media that could be misconstrued. But she knew he was working hard. She suspected he worked *too* hard.

Yet again she rubbed her wrist, missing being able to see the time. She'd bike to the villa and pick it up after taking Alex a pastry from her morning shift.

A few hours later she cycled to the villa. As she punched in the security code, she heard a car slowing behind her. Her pulse spiked—was Rafael home?

She turned, but it wasn't his flashy fast car. It was a sedate number and the driver's window wound down as she watched.

'Good afternoon.'

It was the man who'd mislaid his father the other day. Rafael's nephew. His father was seated in the passenger seat of the flash car that had pulled up outside the secured gates. She chilled, despite the warmth of the afternoon and her ride. If she was right, these people had been horrendous to Rafe.

'Hello.' Her small smile was automatic, but her pulse was thundering. 'May I help you?'

'You're going into the Villa Rosetta?' he asked.

'Yes.' She refused to babble, but she was supernervous.

'You work there?'

She shouldn't be bothered by his assumption that she was hired help, but she didn't correct him.

'My name's Maurice. You remember my father Leonard from the other day? You helped him.'

'Of course I remember.'

'My father would like to see the villa one last time,' Maurice said quietly. 'He's unwell. This is the last time he'll make it to Italy.'

Gracie glanced at the passenger seat of the car and saw the distant look in the older man's eyes. It was a look she recognised. He was stuck in another time—in fragments of memories. Her sympathy rose for him.

'Yes, I understand,' she said quietly. 'But I can't let you in—'

'Just the gardens,' Maurice interrupted. 'He only wants to see the gardens. Not go inside the villa, of course. He used to stay there years ago when he was a boy.'

So Maurice *was* Rafael's nephew and the old man his half-brother. She bit her lip, feeling both dread and empathy.

'He has wonderful memories of the place—or at least he used to,' Maurice said. 'Sometimes those memories are the only ones he can recall. This is his last chance to walk in the gardens again. We're leaving Italy in a couple of days. We tried to contact the new owner for permission but were unsuccessful.'

Of course they had been. Rafe never would have taken his call. Did Rafe even know Leonard was sick?

She hesitated, torn, because she knew exactly what it was like to wish for a few moments of lucidity to have a moment of remembrance with an old man. But this was Rafael's place. And he wouldn't want them here.

'Please.'

Gracie looked into the car at Leonard again and saw just how frail the old man was. Frailer than Alex.

Rafael was away and she could explain it to him—the man was old and sick and surely he'd feel the compassion she did? Rafael had been hurt, but he was still human. Surely he could forgive this ill old man? It was only a small request.

She turned to Maurice. 'Just five minutes, okay? *Five.*'

'Thank you.'

She opened the gate and cycled up the driveway ahead of their car. While Maurice parked she leaned her bike against one of the pillars.

'Is it the roses he remembers?' Gracie asked as Maurice walked around the car to open the door for his father.

'I'm not sure,' Maurice answered gruffly. 'There's not a lot he seems to remember at all.'

She nodded and stepped back as the old man emerged from the car.

'Shall we walk through the roses, Father?'

They had just walked to the lawns when a frosty voice sliced through the warm air.

'May I help you?'

Gracie froze in horror and slowly turned. He was standing on the edge of the grass. He looked impeccable—and impregnable. His dark grey suit was like perfectly tailored armour. And the aggression in his stance, his eyes, his voice rippled through the air.

'Rafael,' she croaked. 'I didn't realise you were back.'

Why hadn't he been in touch already? Why hadn't she thought to tell him of the incident in the *pasticceria* the other morning? But she'd been distracted—by him—at the time.

'Clearly.' He glared at her, anger apparent in every part of him. He didn't say anything to the men standing beside her.

She understood then that his relationship with his half-brother was so broken they couldn't even speak politely about nothings, couldn't stand to be in the same space. They were unable to push beyond the hurt of the past.

'These men wanted to see the grounds before they leave Italy. It's the last opportunity—'

'It's okay,' Maurice interrupted her. 'We'll leave.' He was actually flushed. 'We didn't mean to intrude, Rafael. I wouldn't have had I known you were in residence. I believed you weren't home.'

Wincing internally, Gracie glanced at Rafe. He

shot a look back at her—accusation stabbing from his eyes.

'Your father is already intruding,' he said stiffly.

Gracie turned to look. Leonard had already walked past the path towards the roses and was slowly walking towards the boat shed.

'Father?' Maurice hurried after him.

The old man was moving surprisingly swiftly now, and even from this distance Gracie could hear him muttering.

Rafael wasn't looking at her but she could feel the emotion coming off him in waves. He stalked silently after the men. For a moment she wavered indecisively. But it didn't feel right to leave them alone. She needed to explain to him how this had happened.

Leonard had got as far as the boat shed. He opened the door before Rafe could say anything or stop him. Gracie hurried in after him. Leonard was staring at the vintage speedboat she and Rafe had taken out the other day. It felt like for ever ago now.

'Rosabella,' he said quietly.

Maurice looked astounded as he walked the length of the shed to read the name on the back of the boat—where Leonard couldn't see.

'He remembers the boat?' He shook his head.

'Rosabella.' The smile on Leonard's face was huge. He said nothing else, just happily sat and stroked the smooth hull.

* * *

Rafael knew within two minutes that his half-brother Leonard was extremely unwell. He'd hardly spoken and clearly hadn't recognised him and there was a vacant look in his eyes that revealed more than mere forgetfulness. This was disease.

Bitterness burned. He should have felt pleasure that he was the one who owned the place. That they should've asked his permission when they'd denied him everything. Even when he'd pretended to himself that he didn't care, he still did. He'd wanted this power for so long. He wanted all the experiences that he'd never had. The fun. The laughter. His father.

He wanted everything that they'd withheld from him.

Raw resentment descended with the realisation that even now he was cheated—his half-brother couldn't remember anything, couldn't tell him anything, even if they had been on better terms. Disappointment dissolved his bones like acid. But it wasn't even them who had hurt him this time. It was Gracie.

'Take as long as you like,' he said roughly. He stalked out of the boat shed, unable to watch any more.

Ten minutes later Leonard and Maurice emerged, Gracie walking a pace behind them. Betrayal swept over him. It was so severe he simply couldn't stand to look at her.

'Thank you,' Maurice said stiltedly. 'I know you weren't expecting us. You understand Leonard is—'

'I get it,' he snapped.

'Okay.' Maurice cleared his throat. 'But thank you again.' He turned away but suddenly swung back. 'Roland loved this place too. He'd be pleased you're looking after it.'

Rage stained his vision red. He didn't want or need this man's approval. He didn't need him to say what his father would have liked—he already knew his father would be pleased he owned the place. It had been the dream of theirs—an old man and a young boy, dreaming of a beautiful lake and gelato, of all things...

Rafe just knew there was a pleading look in Gracie's eyes as his nephew spoke but he said nothing more. He didn't dare, fearing the emotion swirling within would spew forth like a fountain. He couldn't risk that. He never wanted them to know they still had any kind of power over him. He refused to care.

Not quickly enough, the men walked to the car. Unable to bear it, Rafe strode to the lake.

The fury that rose in him as he heard her step behind him was too much. He whirled to face her. She had her hands on her hips and her chin tilted high, like a warrior princess ready to defend her territory.

'I didn't know you were home,' she said. 'I

thought…' She trailed off as she realised what she'd been about to say.

'You thought you could get away with it,' he finished for her coldly. Would she have lied to him always? 'Would you *ever* have told me? Could you ever have been *honest*?' he snarled. 'You went behind my *back*.'

And with *him*—Leonard. The half-brother who'd rejected him, who'd denied him his father's name, denied his blood, who'd banished his mother and turned his back on her when she'd needed help. Who'd bullied Rafe for *years*. All the hurt that he'd thought he'd buried burst back as if it had just happened.

'It wasn't planned. It wasn't deliberate,' she said quickly. 'They pulled up at the gate when I arrived. I didn't know what to do.'

'And why did you arrive?' he snapped, drawing his own conclusions. 'Because you'd met them before today. You planned this.'

She paled, but she didn't walk away. 'I did meet them. Leonard wandered past the café early the other morning. He was clearly lost. I sat him down and gave him a drink. I couldn't ignore him when he's clearly unwell.'

All those years ago Leonard had ignored *him*—when he'd been a vulnerable child. Then Leonard had gone on to do worse than ignore him.

'But I didn't plan this,' Gracie continued. 'I came

because I left my watch here the other day and it's irritating me not to have it. It was coincidence that they were outside when I arrived.'

Rafe didn't believe in coincidences. And Gracie obviously got the message because her face flushed.

'Believe me or don't, Rafe, but I'm being honest,' she said. 'And that man is dying. No fight is worth denying someone their dying wish.'

He'd never felt this cold—it was a relief, because all that old agony that he hated might hopefully freeze too. He loathed the truth she spoke. He couldn't bear to have all this history dredged up.

'He denied my mother's dying wish,' he said harshly. He'd denied almost every damn wish of Rafe's for a decade.

But it was Gracie he was most angry with now. Gracie, who'd let that monster in. Gracie, who stood there looking so beautiful and soft and caring. 'Please leave.'

'Rafe?'

'Leave. *Now*,' he shouted. He needed to be alone. He turned back to the villa. Only, he couldn't bear the sight of it right this second. He turned back again and she was there, right in front of him when he'd been ripped open by a rusted knife. He was nothing but jagged edges and oozing blood.

'I'm not leaving when you're this upset,' she said gently.

'I'm not upset,' he spat at her. 'I'm livid.'

'He's an ill old man,' she answered calmly. 'What can he do to you now?'

It wasn't *now*… It was everything. *Rafe* had everything, but still had *nothing*.

'He *exists*!' he yelled rawly.

She looked up at him. It was hot and he was cold and her eyes were so soft, so full of empathy and emotion and infinite patience. And somehow he tumbled into that tenderness.

'They denied *my* existence. My name. He had everything I didn't. Legitimacy. Parents. And he wouldn't even let me have mine. When he was a child, he had both his parents. I didn't. He came here with Dad year after year. He had all those *memories* that I never got the chance to make.'

'And now he's losing them,' she said quietly.

'I know.' His voice cracked. 'He can't even share *them*. He couldn't share anything with me *ever*.' He groaned. 'Do you blame me for hating him for that?'

She shook her head.

'My father promised to bring me here,' he said. 'He said I'd love it. That we'd go on the water together. It was our dream…'

'But you never got to come.'

He breathed out. 'Stupid,' he muttered. 'As if being here could bring him back.' He couldn't bear to look at her. He turned to the lake, blinded by stinging tears that wouldn't fall.

'Because that's what you wanted.' She wound her arms around his waist.

'I said I wanted this villa to add to my portfolio but really it was to prevent Maurice from getting it. And, yes, I got some petty pleasure from that. But I didn't know about Leonard's health. And it wasn't *really* why I wanted it.' He blinked rapidly.

'You loved your father.' She placed her hand over his chest, feeling the pounding of his heart. 'And he died. Then so did your mother.'

He bent his head. 'Yes.'

'And that sucks.'

He turned, seeing her half-shy, half-worried expression. Suddenly that agony eased—just as he admitted its depth.

'It does.' He dragged in another breath. 'What they did to my mother was unforgivable. I never would have let them in here, Gracie. If you had any understanding of me, you would have known that.'

'I know that you're amazingly strong—'

'Don't. Don't put this on me—don't try to make me the bigger person. Because I'm not. You did the wrong thing.'

'Maybe I did,' she said softly. 'But with the right intentions. And you *are* the bigger person. You're not like them, Rafe, that's the whole point. You would never do what they did to you, not to anyone. Not even them.'

He stilled, hating her words. Because she was right.

'They saw you as a threat,' she said. 'And people do dumb things when they're scared. Sometimes people are just mean. But you're not.'

He'd wanted to be. The only reason he hadn't been was because of her. Because *she* wasn't. Yet she'd suffered too. Hugely. How had she stayed so lovely, so forgiving, in the face of all that upheaval?

'Life isn't black and white,' she whispered. 'There's no way of keeping things simple. There's just complication.'

'I didn't mean to make this a pity fest.' He winced. 'You didn't have it easy either.'

'No. Both my parents said they loved me. But if they really loved me, would they have treated me like a bone to be buried and hidden so the other couldn't find me?' She shook her head. 'To be pulled between the two for years? It hurt all of us. As I said, people do dumb things when they're scared.'

Yeah.

He rolled his shoulders—conflicted between ease and discomfort. He didn't know why he'd been so angry only moments ago. Why he'd thought they could still hurt him. He wasn't eight years old and alone now. He was an adult and he had everything he'd never had then—security, certainty. His half-brother showing up shouldn't have bothered him all that much. Yet it had.

'You were kind to Leonard,' he said. 'You're a better person than me, Gracie James.'

'My grandfather is called James,' she said quietly. 'He's similar to Leonard in that his mind was going… I recognised it in Leonard and that's why I felt sorry for him and for Maurice. It's hard.'

Rafael watched her. 'How's your grandfather now?'

'By the time I got back to London, to be able to see him again, his memories were mostly gone. He didn't know who I was. He passed away a year ago. It's his watch I wear.'

No wonder she'd had sympathy for Leonard, then.

'I took the name James as my surname when I decided to start over. I wanted to choose.'

'Because being in charge of your life is important to you,' he said. She'd chosen who she wanted to be—literally. 'I understand that now.'

'Yes.'

'You missed out on so much.'

'So did you,' she replied.

He held her close. With that simple hug, a calm serenity flowed, pushing the remaining angry wreckage further away from his heart. 'Let's go inside and find your watch,' he suggested quietly.

'I'd like that.'

It was in his bedroom. His heart thumping, he picked up the watch with its round face and worn, canvas strap.

'Vintage again.' He tried to smile.

'Bits of history.' She fastened the strap with a small smile. 'It's probably cheesy, but I think they link us—to people, to our pasts. Some building blocks of identity. Maybe that's what you wanted with this villa?'

'Maybe.'

Gracie walked over and framed his face with her hands. Her heart ached for him. He hadn't wanted her to see his vulnerability. His hurt. And she'd just hurt him.

'Don't feel sorry for me,' he said.

'Don't you feel sorry for me either.' She smiled.

She had nothing to give him except herself. Her love. Her honesty. But he didn't want it. There was no point trying to change him. There was only the moment to enjoy.

'I hate how it feels,' he said a little roughly.

'How what feels?'

'This confusion.' He eyed her meditatively. 'It was easier when I could just hate them.'

She smiled up at him. 'Nothing is ever simple.'

He shook his head and brushed his finger across her lips. 'This feels simple. This feels good.'

Gracie didn't reply. While she was glad he was

no longer angry with her, glad he was holding her close again, she was sorry that he was calling time on this conversation. Because this didn't feel all that simple to her.

He turned away from her and went to the luggage he'd stacked just inside the door. 'I brought you a present from Paris.' He held up his hand to forestall any protest. 'Not an emerald bracelet.'

'I should hope not.'

He cocked his head, reading her awkwardness. 'It's only little. Really not that amazing.' He suddenly laughed. 'You really don't like gifts? You probably won't even use it.'

She pulled the package from the carrier bag and pulled apart the tissue wrapped around it.

'It's a rotary pastry cutter,' he explained. 'As I said, not anything fancy but I thought you might like it. Not just vintage, practically antique.' He studied it for a second and his smile was a little lopsided. 'Though I realise now that the vintage things you collect are for their connections to your people, not the things themselves.'

'And the connection of this is to you.' She beamed at him as she turned the cutter over in her hand. 'I love it. Thank you.'

'Really? You love it.' He put his hand to his heart in an amazed gesture.

'You must think I'm so ungrateful.' She winced. Rafe leaned against the wall and regarded her, suddenly solemn. 'No, I think you struggle with being given things.'

Her lungs froze. 'I'm no saint, Rafe.' She sat on the edge of his bed and played with the small handle of the pastry cutter. 'You know I went to stay with my father when I was eighteen...' She drew in a breath to brace herself. 'It was quite a...celebration, I guess. There was a big welcome party. He'd kept presents for me—for all the birthdays and Christmases we'd been apart.' She cleared her throat and looked down at her feet. 'It was so kind...'

'But?' Rafe prompted.

She didn't want to say anything more, it was wrong.

'It's okay to be honest, Gracie. You know you can tell me anything.'

She glanced up at him and saw the acceptance in his eyes. 'It was really sweet,' she said softly. 'It wasn't his fault—he didn't know me and I didn't know him and that hurt us both.'

'The presents were...not your thing?'

She winced. 'They were...'

'Be honest,' he encouraged softly.

'Not all...my thing. But that wasn't a surprise, though, right?' she pointed out, eager to defend her father still. 'How could he know what I liked when we'd been kept apart for so long? Neither of us knew the other. I'm sure I did things that he wasn't a huge fan of.'

'And you couldn't laugh about it?'

She shook her head. She'd never been able to laugh about much with either of her parents. 'The problem was that he kept buying me presents.'

'Impersonal presents,' Rafe noted.

Yes.

Gracie looked at the little pastry cutter in her hands. How was it that Rafe had got her something that she *loved* after knowing her for such a short time? But he'd paid attention to her, he'd taken the time to hunt it out, he'd put real thought into it, not simply ordered the number one most popular gift idea online, irrespective of whether it would suit her or not.

'I asked him not to, told him over and over that he didn't *have* to,' she said urgently. 'That he didn't need to feel like he owed me in that way, that he didn't need to buy my affection… I'm not like that, Rafe.' She looked up at him earnestly. 'I don't care about *things* in that way.' She'd had to travel with so little for so long, she had a great awareness of what was truly of value.

'Anyone who knows you would know that, Gracie.'

Anyone who'd *bothered* to get to know her. And that was the point, of course. She sent Rafe a sad smile, he was so astute.

'My father kept buying, kept *paying*, but I wanted his *time*, not his money. Not things. I wanted…'

She trailed off and tried to put it concisely. 'I saw him with my half-brothers and I wished…'

'You'd had him all your life,' Rafe finished for her.

'Then one day he said he had a big surprise for me. He made such a show of it with everyone there. He'd taken out a lease on a little bakery.' She brushed her hair back. 'It was only small but in a really hip neighbourhood. A whole actual café.'

She glanced up and saw the small frown pleating Rafe's brow.

'Amazing, right?' she said, burning, bitter tears filling her eyes. 'You'd think there'd be nothing better than that for me.' And it should have been. She should have been overwhelmed with gratitude. 'It had been so incredibly generous. So supportive.' A tear slid down her cheek but Rafe didn't move any closer, didn't take his gaze off hers for a second. 'But there was a small apartment in it upstairs. For me. I was to move out of their home and into there alone. Immediately.'

They hadn't wanted her any more.

'But weren't you living with him so he could get to know you and catch up on all those years you were apart?' Rafe asked.

Her throat clogged painfully. 'His boys were young and he was busy with them and his wife… He promised me he wouldn't go after Mum. He said he was sorry and that he loved me but that it wasn't working... I guess it got too much.'

It had come as such a shock. She hadn't been the daughter he'd wanted. They'd missed years and years and they could never get them back, and once she was finally there, he hadn't wanted her to stay.

'I tried so hard,' she said, still so hurt. 'I made the boys my doughnuts, I got them to test all my new flavours. I'd been studying at a culinary arts school, but I tried to fit in, I offered to babysit, I tried to help her around the house... But they were busy, you know? They didn't need me.'

They had their new happy life and she didn't fit. So they'd engineered a way to get her out.

Rafe lifted away from the wall and walked over, hunching down so he could look into her eyes. 'You shouldn't have had to do things to be *needed*, Gracie. You should have just been loved. Just as you are.'

Gracie's body turned to jelly. She quickly put the pastry tool on the bed before she dropped it. She'd *wanted* to be loved. She'd wanted to be in that big, warm house and been welcome. She'd wanted to be safe and secure and been able to stay. She'd wanted a home and a family, finally and for ever...

Rafe waited but she still couldn't speak. 'So you didn't take the lease on the café?'

She vehemently shook her head. 'Of course not.' The misery broke free. 'That's *never* what I wanted from him. But he didn't want me there any more. None of them did.' Tears splashed down her cheeks as she sobbed. 'So I left.'

'For Europe?'

She nodded, furiously wiping away tears, but more kept tumbling. 'It's awful, isn't it? To be so ungrateful for such a gesture?'

'Not awful.'

She closed her eyes so she couldn't see the tenderness in his. Because, no, it was awful. 'It's okay.' She dragged in a steadying breath and tried to pull back her usual calm. 'It's stupid to be upset.'

Rafe covered her cold hands with his. 'It's not stupid,' he said firmly. 'And it's not okay.' He squeezed her fingers gently. 'He thought he was giving you everything but starved you of what you wanted most. Both your parents did that.' He sighed and ran his hand through her hair. 'And that sucks, Gracie. That just sucks.'

He'd used her word to describe it. He was right. And she couldn't see again for crying. She felt his arms go about her and he pressed her close, letting her lean on him, letting her cry against his chest in comfort. And she cried and cried and cried.

'Oh, Rafe, I'm *so* sorry,' she snuffled a long while later.

'Don't be.' His answering caress, the warmth in his tone? It was too soft, too understanding.

She made herself draw back, wiping her eyes again to study him. He steadily, silently regarded her too. He was so unfairly handsome and his gift was lovely but what was even more unfair was his *thought* for her. He knew her better—understood what she liked—more than anyone else in her life ever had. Right now there were still those bruised shadows in his eyes, remnants of the hurt and confusion from his own complicated family. But there was tenderness and understanding too and something else warm and deep swirling in the mix. A kind of silent support and solidarity in the acknowledgement that sometimes, yes, things sucked.

But some things were simple. And how she felt now was very, very simple. Rubbing her fingers on his shadowed jaw, she leaned forward and kissed him.

He leaned back a moment later. 'You're rewarding me for…?'

'Nothing. This isn't for the gift. Not because you were nice to those people, even when you didn't want to be. Not because I've missed you like crazy. The reason I kissed you is so much simpler than that.'

'Oh?'

'You're hot,' she muttered, needing to bring this

back to the light, adult tease it had been from the beginning. 'And you're a great kisser.'

But it wasn't the real reason. It was *everything* about him and she couldn't maintain that easy flirtation. He mattered. And she needed to show him that. She needed to hold him.

He didn't smile as he looked down at her. Intense edginess tightened his features. 'Gracie—'

'Yes,' she answered, before knowing what his question even was.

'I need you, Gracie,' he said roughly.

'Good.' Because she needed him too. She needed him *now*.

She moved quickly, pulling at his belt as she kissed him, suddenly desperate to feel him against her completely. For him to fill her and make her feel that wonderful physical freedom again.

'No,' he said forcefully, suddenly spinning her and pushing her so she fell right back onto the bed. He followed, and grabbing her wrists he pinned her arms above her head, covering her body with his own. 'Not fast. Not this time, Gracie.'

She gasped as sensation rippled down her, making her wriggle beneath him. 'It feels fast to me.'

'No.' He bent and kissed her, learning her mouth again with a slow, luscious sweep of his tongue. 'I'm taking my time.'

He wasn't teasing. He was torturing. Slowly he stripped her bare. Slowly he touched every secret, soft part of her with such tender, caressing focus it bordered on cruelty. Because she was alight and aching and she needed him. There with her—all the way there. Now. She arched—smiling as she screamed, tears tumbling as his power made her tremble.

'No,' he said harshly. 'Not yet, Gracie.'

So she fought back—to know him. To make him feel as raw and exposed and as *wanted* as she did. They rolled together, thrashing out the passion in long, rough sweeps of hands and mouths, breath mingling, bodies straining.

'Rafe. *Please.*'

Finally he gave her what she truly wanted—himself. His body invaded hers—fiercely dominant, ferocious, he clamped his arms around her. Searing, slow, sublime. She shook in total rapture. They were so close nothing could come between them—nothing *was* between them. Only pleasure. Only adoration. Only *love*.

It took a long time for her to come back to reality. When she did, he was slumped over her, still breathing hard, spent.

Emotion swamped her. The most intense emotion of her life. It wasn't gratitude, or greed…it was something she had to give to him. Something she could no longer keep contained.

'Rafe…' She rubbed her fingertips over his roughened jaw. 'I—'

'Don't say it, Gracie,' he whispered harshly in her ear. 'Don't.'

She stilled. 'I have to be honest. I won't hide how I feel about you.'

He lifted his head and looked into her eyes. 'You don't feel anything.'

Shocked, she dropped her hand. 'You don't get to deny me—my voice, my feelings, my life. I would share it all with you, Rafe. You know I would.'

'Don't—'

'I've fallen in love with you.' She blurted it.

'Adoration,' he said, pulling back from her. 'That's all. You said it yourself.' He released a harsh sigh and vaulted off the bed, scooping up a towel.

'You know it's not that.'

He turned back to face her, his expression remote. 'I can't give you what you want.'

'What makes you think I want anything from you?' She lifted her chin. 'Perhaps I just want to give.'

'Everybody wants something. There's always a price.'

Oh, that hurt. 'Not for love. Real love is unconditional, Rafe. Real love just *is*. You can't stop it. You can't deny it.'

He glared at her. 'Would you just let me take and take and take from you? You'd let me have all your goodness, all your energy, all your generosity until I'm sick of it and cast you aside? You'd settle for that? No.' He shook his head. 'You wouldn't. You wouldn't even come to Paris with me for a few days.'

She sat up and curled her arms around her knees. 'I offer my love. I don't expect you to love me back. But I do expect you to respect my feelings. Not to deny them. And, no, I understand that you don't want what I'm offering. So I'll not "settle". I know that when I walk out the door today, it's goodbye. I know it's over.'

'Then why say it?' he asked in pure frustration. 'I don't want this to be over. Not like this. Not yet.' He shook his head. 'Why couldn't you have left it unsaid?'

'Because I *won't* hide. I won't deny. I won't keep secrets. Because I do deserve more.' She angled her head and *fought*. 'And so do you. You just don't believe you do.'

'It doesn't exist, Gracie. The happy-ever-after you want is a fantasy. Fairy tales are not real.'

'*Emotions* are real, Rafe.' She got off the bed and grabbed her clothes, holding them in front of her.

'Really? You're lecturing me on facing emotions? The woman who spends her life pretending everything is perfect? Who can't admit to her boss when she's too tired to work because she's scared of letting her down and losing her friendship?'

Oh, that was low.

'You live in this fairy-tale world,' he continued harshly. 'But you're still scared to be anything but happy and glad as if the world here is the most perfect place. You say you're honest. But you're not. And the person you're not honest with is yourself.'

His attack stunned her. 'I just opened up to *you*.' She was so hurt. 'But because I've dared to admit that I care about you, you're now turning on me? What—must there be something wrong with me if I love you? You're more broken than I thought. Do you truly think someone can't possibly love you?'

An undefined emotion kindled in his eyes, something even stronger than the anger she'd seen in him before.

'I can never be the person you want me to be, Gracie. I never had the kind of home you dream of. I look around the villa and to me it's all empty rooms with the possibility of paying guests. The world you want is alien to me. I don't want links—chains—to the past.'

He was lying. Pushing her away. Punishing her for what she'd just said. Wasn't he?

'And yet you bought this villa,' she said.

'It was a good business opportunity.'

'And that's all?'

'No. It was the *remnants* of a childhood fantasy. It wasn't real. It didn't bring me happiness. Relationships, memories, trinkets, they don't do that.

Freedom does that for me. Financial freedom. And emotional. I need to be free, Gracie. I can't bear the burden of your happiness.'

His words completely cleaved her. That wasn't what she wanted either—and her anger flared. 'I'm not asking you to do that. All I've done is tell you how I feel and, of course, you can't handle that. I expect *nothing* from you.' She stepped back. 'Give me some space so I can finish getting dressed.'

He left the room immediately.

She sat back on the bed, drawing in a strangled breath. She'd known, hadn't she? This was why she'd refused his invitation to Paris—because what was nothing but easy to him was so much more meaningful to her.

When she went downstairs ten minutes later, he was lingering near the front door. 'I've been thinking—'

'How novel,' she interrupted curtly.

He folded his arms across his chest and sent her a look. 'I can get someone else to cater for the party.'

'You're taking away the contract from us?' Her eyes narrowed. 'Because you and I aren't sleeping together any more? Because I dared tell you how I feel about you?'

'Don't bring the personal into this.'

She stared at him, shocked at his gall. 'You're

the one who can't separate business from personal. You want to punish me for caring?'

'No,' he answered softly. 'I don't want to hurt you any more than I have.'

Pride made her want to lie, to deny he'd hurt her at all. But then he'd win. He'd be another person affecting her so much she was no longer true to herself. She wasn't going to hide her emotions. Not from him.

'You can't,' she said simply. 'I'm hurt, Rafe. You've already hurt me as much as it's possible for me to hurt. But by doing this you're hurting my co-workers as well. You're hurting my friend, my employer and her bottom line. I can hold it together. I'm not going to have a tantrum or look at you with tearful eyes.' She walked past him to the door. 'Go score another woman. Whatever you want. I won't be watching you. I'm capable of doing my job because I'm a professional and I can control my emotions. The question is, are you?'

'This is the way you want to play it?'

'I'm not playing anything. I'm being honest. I want to do my job. You're leaving Bellezzo, but it's my home. I'm not going anywhere. I'd like the contract.'

'If that's what you want.'

'It is,' she said with dignity. 'We're halfway through the preparations and you won't get anything as good as what we can provide in this short time frame. I'm sure you wouldn't want to starve your guests.'

He was very still. 'I don't want you serving the food,' he gritted.

That she could be even more hurt by him was a shock. 'I'll be sure to stay hidden in the kitchen,' she said in a strangled voice.

'That wasn't what I—' He bit off whatever he was going to say and a look of absolute frustration contorted his face. 'Let me give you a lift back into the village.'

She'd recovered her emotion again—just. 'No, thanks.'

'Gracie.' He stepped after her.

'I can't stay to chat longer. I need to get home before it gets dark. This Red Riding Hood shouldn't have strayed so far from the path, should she? There's a wolf in these woods. That'll teach me for living in my perfect, fairy-tale world.'

CHAPTER TWELVE

Rafe walked along the lakefront, looking back at the villa that was currently being decorated by a team of lighting and sound experts. He'd only arranged the stupid party in the first place to have an excuse to see Gracie again. What a fool. He should have called it off and left Italy already.

Except he hadn't been able to do that to Gracie and Francesca. Gracie had been right when she'd taken him to task the other day. They'd worked too hard, they'd got in the supplies needed. Of course, he could have just paid for it all, but it wasn't about the money. It was the impression and the connections they could make. He wanted that for them. They deserved it. It was one little thing he could actually give her. Because what she'd *said* she wanted was impossible.

He was still furious with her for ruining what had been a perfectly suitable arrangement. Everything had been great. He'd been happy. She'd been happy. But it hadn't been enough for her. Even when he'd warned her. He'd told her right at the start and she'd said she was okay with what he could offer her. She'd *lied*. Her declaration of love had been a betrayal of that honest arrangement between them. And then her damn dignity?

How was it possible that he'd insulted her—he'd completely rejected her—and yet she still saw what she believed to be the best in him? Her hope, her optimism was unsinkable. He was even more furious with her. What made it worse was that he still wanted her.

'Mr Vitale.'

'Alex.' He turned in surprise. 'I wasn't expecting to see you.'

His team had flown in two days ago and taken over the arrangements. He'd holed up in the large study and pretended he wasn't even in Italy. He hadn't expected to see any of the Bellezzo residents until the party. He'd wanted it that way.

'I wanted to ensure everything looked right for tonight,' Alex explained. 'I was able to convince your new security to let me in.' Alex paused. 'And I wanted to give you something.'

'Oh?' Rafe didn't trust the old man's bland expression.

'I've been crafting new roses for years. It's both hobby and career. This perfect bloom is mine.' He held out the rose.

Rafael had no option but to take it from him.

'If it suits, I'm going to plant it all along the eastern access pathway.'

'Of course. I appreciate your skill, Alex.'

'It's called Aurora Grace. Aurora was my wife, the most beautiful woman you ever saw.'

'That's lovely.' Rafe tried to walk away because he really didn't want to hear any more. But Alex walked with him.

'I chose Grace because the plant is generous to a fault. She has abundant petals and abundant roses. She keeps blooming even when it's not in her best interests for her own survival, but she just keeps on giving.'

Rafe stopped and stared at the old man in silence. But his glare just bounced off the man.

'She needs some special care,' Alex added.

Talk about laying it on thick. But he couldn't hate the man for it, it was oddly good to know Gracie had someone in her corner. She didn't deserve to be alone.

'Then the plant is very lucky to have you to tend it. The whole garden is. I appreciate it.' Rafe spoke through gritted teeth. 'You should probably know I've decided to sell the villa, it doesn't fit with the rest of my portfolio, so I'd like you to continue to maintain the roses until the new owner takes control.'

'Of course.' Alex's expression toughened. 'It's a pleasure for me to care for it. I don't consider it hard work. Not work at all.'

Rafe turned his back on the pointed tone. Hard work? Gracie James was the easiest woman in the world for anyone normal to love. She ought to be nestled in the centre of a loving family with all the security that she craved. She needed someone strong to create that for her. She needed a man who could give her everything. Rafe could give her money, travel, jewels but she didn't want those. She wanted the one thing he couldn't give. His heart was too shrunken and scarred for her to have. It wasn't enough. *He* wasn't enough. She deserved more than what he could offer. So he'd get out of her way.

The problem was, she was there. In the villa, permeating the walls with her gorgeous scent, with her mouth-watering skills—both pastry and personal. She made him want. His assistant had been surprised by his request to use the local bakery for the food. But he'd known she could do it.

Over eighty guests descended on his peace. Catering staff poured champagne. The DJ from LA sent good beats echoing across the lake. And Gracie James gave every damn guest's taste buds an orgasm.

He was furious with her for stripping herself back so openly and pushing him into craving something he'd never wanted. He'd never wanted to think about her all the time. He'd never wanted to feel guilty. He'd never wanted to miss her. He'd never wanted to wonder if he'd been *wrong*.

And now she was there—where he could see her. Smiling as she served her pastries. She was wearing a very simple, discreet black dress. As if she could somehow blend into the background?

He stalked his way through the crowd to talk to her.

'There aren't enough serving staff,' she explained coolly as soon as she saw him.

'It's fine,' he snapped.

But it wasn't fine. He hated seeing other people looking at her, talking to her. Worse still, asking *him* who she was. He watched as she went back down the hallway and he saw one of the damn fashion photographers follow her.

When he got to the kitchen, she was putting a final few pastries on a loaded platter and the photographer was leaning on the counter near her and laughing.

'Only catering staff are allowed in here,' he said sharply. 'Not guests.'

The man raised his eyebrows. 'Sorry, Rafe.' But the smile he sent Gracie wasn't apologetic at all.

'Was that necessary?' She turned on him once the photographer had left. She looked pale, that ready smile didn't spring to her lips for him any more. 'He was only being polite.'

The guy wasn't being polite. He had been making a play for her.

Rafe soaked up the emotion swirling in her eyes. But he couldn't figure out what it was. Hurt. Defiance. Anger. Pride? All of that. And now he felt a heel.

She shouldn't have come. He shouldn't have stayed.

'I'm sorry,' he said gruffly.

'Only because you feel guilty. But you don't need to feel guilty.' Her lips curved in a bright, meaningless smile. 'Get over yourself, Rafe. There's more to my life than *you*. So much more. Even here in my sleepy village where I'm buried and wasting my life.'

He grimaced at her echo of his insult. 'I'm sorry.'

'You've already said that.' She lifted the tray and took it to the doorway, meeting one of the waitresses in the hallway before returning. 'That was the last lot we have, so I'm done. Francesca will get our things in the morning.'

Gracie had made the best damn pastries ever, not for Francesca and the business but purely to spite Rafael. To prove that even though she was hurt, she was not wrecked. Never wrecked. And she'd succeeded. She'd had people coming up to her all night, complimenting her. Francesca had run out of business cards.

But she didn't feel good. Victory was hollow because she hadn't won what she'd really wanted. She hadn't got *him*.

He'd never put her first. He'd never admit his need…but maybe her thinking he even *did* need her was wishful thinking. Maybe he truly didn't. He already had all these other people running to do his bidding. His life was so far removed from her own simple one. His was high-powered and wealthy and fast.

How could she have thought she'd forged any real kind of emotional connection with him? It had been a couple of weeks. An affair. And in another five minutes he'd forget about her. People always did. They got on with their own lives.

Now he stood silently, watching her wash her hands. She braced to walk away. But she couldn't resist asking whether what she'd heard was true. 'You told Alex you're selling the villa.'

'It seems a good time now the restoration is complete and it's had some publicity. I only bought it out of petty spite to stop Leonard and Maurice from getting it.' He shrugged. 'Turns out they only wanted a last look at it anyway, so it was all a waste of my time. Joke's on me.'

Pain whistled through her bones like an arctic gale. She'd hoped Alex had misunderstood.

'You're back to that line?' she said. 'It wasn't a place that you wanted too?' Hadn't he loved it himself? Hadn't he made memories there that he wanted to keep? Clearly not. He couldn't wait to get away.

He didn't love her. He was only bothered because he thought he'd hurt her and his conscience didn't like that. And despite the humiliation, it was true, he *had* hurt her. But what hurt her most of all was the realisation that *he* was that damaged. That he'd miss out on so much because he couldn't push past his own ingrained defences. But she couldn't fix him. He didn't want to be fixed. He didn't think there was anything wrong with him. And she was furious with herself for being so damn soft where he was concerned.

'You and I don't want the same things,' he said curtly.

'You don't know what you want, and even if you did, you couldn't admit it,' she said, and walked out of the back door—the servants' exit.

'I only want what's best for you,' he called after her angrily.

She turned back, her anger breaking. 'Don't act like you're doing what's best for me. You're doing what's best for yourself, as you always do. You're the biggest coward I've ever met.'

She walked out of the villa and got into Francesca's van. She'd done it. She'd got through the night with her head held high—until now. Now she knew he was leaving for good.

Now she was wrecked.

CHAPTER THIRTEEN

'YOU'RE SURE YOU won't come along?' Alex asked as he started up his old truck. 'The roses are almost over for the season. Don't you want to see the last of them?'

Gracie forced a small smile and shook her head. 'I'll come down in another few weeks and see their winter beauty. I have too much to do for Francesca today.'

Alex waved and drove away and Gracie turned to walk down the narrow street towards the Pasticceria Zullo. It was far too soon to go anywhere near Villa Rosetta. Just over a week since that horrible party and Rafael's departure early the next day.

There'd be another festival next year. She'd be over him by then. The villa would have been sold and a new owner installed. She hoped it would be a family to enjoy it, rather than continuing as a soulless holiday home for the dysfunctional and fortune-stricken. Hopefully Alex would still be tending the roses and she and Francesca would have expanded their empire.

Meantime, she'd plod on as she was, where she was. Heartbreak wasn't going to drive her from the one home she'd chosen for herself. She loved Bellezzo—the warmth, the water, the people, even their kind curiosity. But she was furious for letting memories of Rafael taint her whole town—for doing exactly what she'd promised them both she wouldn't. For falling for him. It wasn't like she'd chosen to. She'd thought she'd had it under control—that it was just a crush that, once indulged, would pass.

It totally wasn't and totally hadn't.

Didn't he need love? Didn't everyone? But he didn't want it from her. Maybe she should have fought harder, but there was only so much rejection a girl could take. Because *she* needed love too.

She'd tried to be honest to others and to be true to herself. But she still didn't have the love or the family that she'd longed for. She still didn't truly fit in. Maybe she'd never truly belong here in Bellezzo either—she didn't even speak the language properly. And it was only her work that had warmed people to her. Despite everything, this still wasn't the *home* she'd been seeking for so long. Maybe she'd never have it.

'Quit it,' she muttered to herself, torpedoing her self-pitying thoughts and walking more quickly to work. 'Do something.'

She was going to be *fine*—in the future. She refused to regret her honesty. Or walking away. He said people settled and maybe some did. But *she* wasn't going to settle for what little he was willing to give her for however long he chose to. She had more self-worth than that. Even if she did regret that fact at two in the morning when she was restless and lonely and wishing she'd never opened her stupid mouth.

At least she knew she *could* love, right? At least she'd had an amazing experience and one day, a long time from now, she might have it again. She might meet someone new—even here, in her sleepy, safe little village where she *wasn't* hiding. Until then, she was just going to have to keep super insanely busy.

But the temptation to flee was strong. Now she understood her mother's need to run from every fear. Her mother had wanted to hold on to her, not share her. But she'd been so afraid of losing her that she'd clung too tight and in the end she'd lost her anyway. Because Gracie had felt like nothing more than a possession. That resentment Gracie felt towards her mother? She never wanted Rafe feeling that towards her. She would never smother or stifle someone she loved. So she couldn't give in to that other instinct warring within her—to follow him and fight harder for him. She'd told him how she felt and what she wanted. His answer, his choice wasn't going to change. She had to accept it, she'd be honest and face her misery, and eventually she would get over it.

One long, slow day at a time.

* * *

Rafe strode down the busy Manhattan street, mentally adding to his to-do list. He was back to business—working on a new acquisition, checking up on other investments, planning further developments—barking orders into his phone. He needed to travel more to personally check on his management team. That would help reignite the passion for his work, wouldn't it?

But at every café he walked past he looked at the pastries and just knew they wouldn't taste as good as hers. Weirdly he didn't feel like eating at all. He had a permanently nauseous feeling in his gut.

He'd been happy—damn it—for years. He'd worked hard, played hard, enjoyed all the finest things in life. Being his own man. And he'd been more than happy with that, hadn't he? He'd loved striving for more.

Except it wasn't giving him satisfaction now. The deals were boring. Another hotel? So what? Another apartment complex? He really didn't give a damn. The drive to conquer had fizzled.

He had to be coming down with a bug. Nothing seemed to soothe the constant nagging sensation in his chest. He wasn't sleeping well either. Not even physical exhaustion led to a full night's sleep and, heaven knew, he'd tried. He'd basically run a marathon the other night and followed it up by swimming an ocean's worth of lengths in the hotel's basement pool. Regardless, he still woke during the night, that ache in his chest exacerbated by the unwanted yearning of his body. His sexual drive burned. That was the one and only part of him still fired up. Hungrier than ever.

Sex.

He'd been having a lot of it with Gracie, so going from feast to famine was an adjustment, right? That was all it was. He could easily make a call and collect a willing bedmate. But the thought of sleeping with someone else made his skin crawl and the thought of Gracie sleeping with someone else made his temper flare. Never had he felt this irritable. Because underneath it all was the rasping desire to see her. Just see her and ensure she was okay.

Of course she'd be okay. It was all just intensity and it would pass. Because how could she love him when she barely knew him? He'd flattered her, he'd made her feel good. It was gratitude she felt. Not love. She'd been lonely—

But denying her declaration wasn't fair to her. She'd been so determined to be honest. What she'd said the other day, she'd meant.

So they wanted different things. And he couldn't take advantage of her feelings when he felt nothing but...

Adoration.

She'd joked about that—teased him with his own platitudes that it would pass. That nothing was permanent. That it was just a crush.

It didn't feel like any other damn crush.

He had no proper experience of love. He didn't really know what it was.

He had nothing to give her—at least, nothing intangible. And it was all about the intangible with Gracie. Not the money, the jet or jewels.

Trust was impossible—he couldn't trust what he was feeling now. This dragging pain? This growing insistence that he'd made a mistake? How could he be sure it wouldn't change or fade or just die? Because Gracie's supposed love for him—couldn't that just die too?

The ache in his chest sharpened to an eye-watering pain. He couldn't bear the thought of her taking away the love she'd declared for him.

Yeah. *That* was what he was afraid of. That she'd stop loving him. That she'd leave him. That he would lose her. To be cast out and alone again? Never. He'd pushed her away before that could possibly happen.

Yes, it had been a short time that they'd been together but what he felt for her—the comfort and ease he felt around her, the laughter and amusement he enjoyed with her, the desire to provoke her that melted into protectiveness, the heat and total loss of control… What was all that if not…what?

But Gracie had been honest. Even when it had cost her, when it had embarrassed her, she had been honest. Could he claim the same? No. He'd backed away—not brave enough to probe his real motivations.

Did it matter?

From the damn heart attack he seemed to be having right now, apparently it did. She was kind, generous, loving, *forgiving*. Maybe the person he really needed to learn from was her. Maybe he'd just hurt the one person who would have always been there for him if he hadn't treated her like dirt. He'd abandoned her. He'd rejected her.

He stopped still on the pavement, murmuring an apology to the person who almost smacked into him from behind. He stepped out of the stream of pedestrians and tried to breathe more deeply, rubbing his chest with the heel of his hand.

'You all right, mister?'

He glanced down. An elderly tourist stopped beside him, a worried look in her eye.

'Uh, yeah.' He inhaled sharply. 'I think I will be.' He conjured up a smile for the old dear. But his smile rapidly turned genuine in appreciation of her thoughtfulness. 'Thank you.'

It was the kind of thing Gracie would do without the slightest hesitation. Because she noticed and she cared and she had a hugely generous soul.

A rush of decisiveness overwhelmed him. He needed to get back to Italy. He needed to make it right—to tell her his truth. Never to be afraid.

It couldn't be too late. He refused to consider it.

CHAPTER FOURTEEN

'A FAMILY IS moving into Rosetta.' Sofia—Alex's minestrone-maker and Francesca's cousin—swept into the *pasticceria* and ignored the queue of people to gossip. 'It's not going to be a holiday villa any more. I just heard from Stella.'

'Oh?' Francesca muttered noncommittally, shooting Gracie a small smile of support.

Gracie kept busy smoothing the custard and pretended she wasn't eavesdropping.

'Apparently they're moving in almost right away.' Sofia added. 'It's happened so quickly they haven't even made the sale listing official.'

Gracie had spent the past week avoiding the Villa Rosetta and avoiding talking much to anyone. She'd even been reduced to entertaining the idea of going away for a week or so, just to avoid the curious glances of the villagers.

So this news was helpful. She was glad a family was moving in. Villa Rosetta was made for a family and she would truly be able to move forward. She'd never see Rafael Vitale again.

But as that realisation struck home she had to turn away. Darting into the back corner of the kitchen, she closed her eyes in a futile attempt to hold back her tears. Because that realisation hurt. Utterly and everywhere.

'Gracie? Gracie?'

She whirled at the concern in Francesca's voice. Giving her cheeks a hurried wipe, she went out. 'What's wrong? Is it Alex?'

She lurched to a halt in the middle of the small café and stared.

Prickling heat washed over her, swiftly chased by cold sweat. She was staring at Rafael Vitale. The man she missed with every breath. The man who'd torn her heart out.

He said nothing. He didn't need to. The rest of the world disappeared.

She couldn't speak. She desperately wanted to flee or hide or curl into a ball and die. But she couldn't get her body to move. She'd been glued in place by his presence. And right this second she hated him for it.

'Gracie,' he said quietly.

She couldn't answer.

'Don't look at me like that, Gracie.'

She had no idea how she was looking at him. Tears were stinging her eyes again and she didn't want blurry vision. She wanted to be able to see him. To believe he was here. Why was he here? Why had he returned?

Emotion broke through the shocked rigidity her defensive system had encased her in.

Anger. Pure, electric anger.

'I made a mistake,' he suddenly said in an uneven voice. 'Huge. More than one. Lots.'

'What are you doing here?' Her throat was so tight she couldn't get her voice past a whisper.

The café was quieter than a mausoleum. Was no one else breathing either?

She couldn't think what to say. Her heart raced, drumming blood in her ears. It was impossible to think. She fell back onto her work, like an automaton. 'You want some pastries? Bread?'

'No. I just want you.'

She was shocked to silence all over again. He couldn't have just said that. She couldn't have this conversation in front of all these people. Clenching her fists, she finally forced her broken-hearted body to move. She stalked away from the concerned gazes of her customers, her boss. And him.

Most of all him.

'Don't run away from me, Gracie,' he called as she burst out the door and into the hot summer air.

'Then don't tear me apart in front of my world,' she snapped back. 'Give me some *privacy.*'

He stilled. 'I'm sorry. I was trying to…'

'To what?'

He stared at her for a moment, then swung round to see the people now standing behind him outside the café. He turned back, hurriedly stepping towards her. 'Privacy. Right.' He gestured to his car. 'Please.'

The Ferrari was illegally parked right across the road from the café.

She stared as he opened the passenger door for her. Was she going to let him do this? Could she really take any more hurt?

I just want you.

She wanted to believe that so much. She wanted *him* so much. But he didn't do relationships of the kind she wanted. He didn't do for ever.

'Please, Gracie.' His voice was soft so only she could hear and she couldn't bear to look into his eyes.

She couldn't bear to deny him. Or herself. Not again. Not ever.

Stiffly she stepped closer so she could get into the car. Except he grabbed her arm and leaned in to whisper, 'I've never had it before, Gracie. I didn't know how to handle it.'

'Handle what?' she croaked.

'Love.'

Her heart thudded so hard it knocked all the air from her lungs and she couldn't get any more in. 'I'm not—'

'I miss you,' he interrupted, his whisper harsher and rushed. 'I hate waking up and you're not there. I hate that I pushed away the best thing ever to enter my life. I hate that I was that stupid to run from this.'

She couldn't resist any more. She looked up to meet his gaze. The dark heat, the bruised look beneath his eyes smote her heart. 'This?'

'You.' His fiery eyes burned into hers. 'I hate the villa without you. It's too big. It's empty. *I'm* empty.'

Her mouth dried. 'But you've sold it.'

'No.' He shook his head in a jerky movement. 'I took it off the market.'

'Sofia just said a family is moving in. Almost immediately.'

He stood very still for a moment. Then he nodded. 'I'm hoping that's what's going to happen.' He drew a deep breath. 'It's not a very big family. Yet. It's a couple. I like to think they'll have some kids eventually.'

'A couple?' She couldn't tear her gaze from his, from the ferocity of his focus on her.

'You and me.'

A whooshing noise fuzzed her hearing—like large waves crashing on the shore. She couldn't keep up with what he was saying. She couldn't believe it. 'You're keeping the villa?'

'Only if you're living in it with me,' he muttered. 'Alex can tend his roses. We'll get him better help. You can work in the *pasticceria*, or you can develop your catering business from the kitchen.'

Her head felt woollier than ever. 'Did you say… kids?'

As he stared into her eyes, his gaze narrowed

and he gently shook her arm a little. 'Get in the car, Gracie. We need privacy.'

She was trembling so much it took two attempts to get her seatbelt clicked. She couldn't get her walloping heart to ease. He didn't speak and she couldn't. She was shaking inside. He couldn't drive fast enough for her. She needed his touch on her again—to feel inside and out that he was here, that he'd come back to her and he wasn't leaving. She didn't want him to leave her ever again. But was that what he'd even meant?

Uncertainty ate away what little security she had.

I just want you.

For what—sex? For another fortnight? Doubts circled like clouds of doom. She wanted to believe in the fairy tale, but *he* was the one who'd told her fairy tales were for fools. She didn't want to be a fool over him. She didn't want to begin to believe…

He screeched to a stop outside the villa, flung his seatbelt off and leaned towards her.

'Trust doesn't come easily for me—loving,' he muttered harshly. 'Except you're so loveable.' He turned her face so she had to look at him. 'You're so easy to love, Gracie. I want you. I want *everything* with you. And I want it for always. Please tell me it's not too late.'

Everything for always? A single fat teardrop slid

down her cheek. She couldn't stand it. 'Of course it's not too late. I can't just switch it off.'

And she was sorry he'd been so hurt that he'd think she could. She gulped back a sob.

'No. Don't cry.' He drew her closer, his whisper urgent. 'I'm sorry. So sorry. How do I make this better?'

He didn't give her time to answer. With a growl he swooped, slamming his mouth on hers—hard and rough and passionate. She clutched him back, moaning under his onslaught, desperately angry and empty and needing to kiss him back to *know*. It was brutal and raw and she couldn't hold back because she'd missed him too much. She poured all her pain into answering his kiss. And suddenly it changed completely—no less wild, but the warmth that began to flood her body was like no other. *Yes.* This was what she needed. To feel his passion—to burn again in the fire that always ignited between them. She couldn't ever get enough.

But he suddenly pulled away from her and shot out of the car. 'Come with me.' He opened her door and took her hand, marching her so fast to the roses she had to run to keep up.

'It should be here,' he said roughly.

'What sh—'

'You said you loved me,' he interrupted her. 'That you wanted me to let you love me. But that's not enough. *You* need love too, Gracie. And I love

you. I want you. I'm not good at it, but I plan to
get better.'

She stared at him, shocked into silence all over
again.

'Did you hear me, Gracie?' he said. 'I love you.
I really love you.'

Her eyes filled all over again. 'Rafe?'

'I know it's not been long, but I need—' He
broke off, and reaching into his pocket he pulled
out a small box.

'Rafe—'

He was on his knee in front of her. 'Please, Gracie, will you marry me?'

She stared at the ring he'd revealed. *'Rafe.'* She
covered her mouth with her hand so she wouldn't
giggle inappropriately, but a gurgle of amusement
snuck out anyway even as another tear rolled down
her cheek. 'It's ridiculously huge.'

'I know, right?' He suddenly smiled up at her
encouragingly. 'It's okay to laugh. I didn't want
anyone mistaking it for anything else.'

'Like what?' She giggled again. 'A container
ship?'

'Not a container ship. An anchor. So you can
look down and know you're safe. That you have a
home with me.'

Her laugh died as her heart melted. More of
those tears sprang to her eyes.

'I know you don't generally like jewellery as

gifts,' he added with a small smile. 'So I thought I'd go all out with just the one item—an outrageously massive diamond that you can wear for ever.'

For ever.

She dropped to her knees to match him and put her finger to his lips. 'No, I love it. I love you. I only laughed because I'm nervous and I'm babbling because it's you and you're really here and you overwhelm me. You know you have from the very first moment I saw you. And I can't believe this is happening. I can't wait to put that massive ring on because then I'll know it might be real. It's the perfect anchor for me. I want to be with you—'

Her hands shook but so did his and it took longer than it should have because they got caught up kissing and touching and tearing off the clothing that blocked them from where they wanted to touch most.

'Missed you,' he muttered hoarsely, hauling her beneath him to press himself home with a sure, sharp thrust. 'So much.'

'Yes,' she cried out as he filled her. Again and again he completed her. And she knew then just how much she was loved. *'Yes.'*

'I'm sorry,' he groaned, gently tracing her swollen mouth a long moment later. 'I'm still recovering from the horror of the last few days. I wanted to do everything right.'

'No one does everything right all the time.' She framed his face with her hands and embraced him with all her body and soul. '*You're* right just as you are. Just you is perfect for me.'

'But I hurt you.'

'You did.' She nodded.

'Yet you still love me.' He looked intensely vulnerable as he said it.

Her heart broke again as she realised how deep his insecurity struck. He'd thought she'd stop loving him because they'd argued? He'd worried that she wouldn't want him any more? But why would he believe in love, in forgiveness when he'd never been shown that before?

'I'll always love you. No matter what.'

'Are you feeling sorry for me?' he growled, nipping her lip. 'I told you I don't want pity—'

'Be quiet. I love you.' She placed her hand over his mouth. 'And I need to show you that I love you too. Do you think you can take it?'

He grunted as she pushed him with all her might so he rolled onto his back on the grass. She rolled too, keeping pace so she lay on top of him. She kissed him again the way she'd ached to for days— moved on him, writhing in pleasure at the feel of his strength beneath her and between her thighs. He was so powerful, so strong. And he was hers.

A low, satisfied laugh escaped him when she finally lifted her head.

'I'm not going to be silent,' he warned her with a teasing smile. 'Because I love you and what you do to me. You're everything to me.'

He swept his arms down her back, helping her ride them home to ecstasy. She planted her palm on his chest so she could feel the wonderfully fast, strong beat of his heart as she rocked faster still, revelling in the pleasure of his body and the passion in his eyes.

'I feel closer to you than I've ever felt to anyone.' He breathed hard. 'I thought I never wanted this. I didn't want to need anyone, ever. But you…' He sighed and swept her hair back so he could kiss her again. 'You're honest and generous and optimistic. I love your infectious enthusiasm for all the little things. And now I love you so much I can't bear the thought of life without you and that freaking terrifies me, Gracie. I don't want to make you unhappy. I'll never ask you to choose me over your home. I get that you need to stay here and I don't care where I live as long as I'm with you. So I can work from here. I'll have to travel sometimes but I can reduce it and you don't have to come. You can stay here and I will always return.'

That he'd make such a massive shift for her was so generous. But it also wasn't entirely fair. 'I thought I was being so in control—you know, choosing my home, my name, my job,' she said sombrely. 'But you were right, I've been running away, *hiding*, pretending everything was fantastic when really it wasn't always. I wanted to make my choice. But *you're* my choice. And I don't want to do what my parents did. I don't want to make you stay only where I say. Yes, I love the villa and I love Bellezzo, but I know you have work commitments and I want to be with *you*, wherever that may be.' She swallowed. 'I don't want to be apart from you.'

'Then we'll work it out. The villa is perfect as our base home, though, right?' He smiled at her. 'It has lots of bedrooms, definitely room for, what was it…four children?'

'You were serious about that?' she whispered. 'You never wanted children.'

'I'll have four if they're yours.' His smile was suddenly wicked. 'I want to see you pregnant. I want to see you showering our children with all the love that I never got. That might just make my heart burst. I know you'll do that for them and I'll do it too because you'll help me. I can learn, I want to learn. And I want my children to have loving siblings. I'll show my sons how a man should love his woman. And you can make anything you want in our kitchen. I want you to have it all.'

'All?' She smiled at him blissfully because he had just given her it *all*. 'I have this fantasy of marrying you here in the rose garden,' she said shyly. 'I have amazing memories attached to those roses.'

'*Caramellina*, there's nothing I'd love more, but the roses are almost over and I'm *not* waiting almost a year to marry you.'

'Then let's do it as soon as possible,' she said with a nervous chuckle. 'I think Alex still has a couple of roses I could carry and I know a bakery where we can get a nice cake.'

'Done,' he answered immediately, his expression intense. 'No getting away from me now, darling.' He suddenly smiled. 'You can't help but be quick.'

'Only when it comes to you.' She shot him a coy look. '*Always* when it comes to you.'

'I think you enjoy slow sometimes.'

Shaking her head, she fluttered her fingers over his stomach, loving the ripple of muscles beneath his hot skin. 'Not this time.'

'Yes, this time.'

He firmly swept his hands down her back and thighs and pulled her to the position he wanted. So exposed, so vulnerable, so *his*. She wriggled but his grip tightened. She stilled and met that gleaming challenge in his eyes. His hands tightened more. Slowly he lowered his head.

'You're so mean,' she moaned.

But he was right. She enjoyed slow. With him, she loved it.

'We should go back into the village to see Alex and Francesca soon,' he said lazily, over an hour later. 'They'll be worried about you.'

Her heart swelled, because she knew he was right. Her friends cared. So did he. 'That would be good. That would be really good.'

She put her head on his chest and closed her eyes in pure delight. She'd found her home, and she knew she'd found his—in each other's heart.

* * * * *

If you enjoyed
Awakening His Innocent Cinderella
you're sure to enjoy these other
Natalie Anderson stories!

Claiming His Convenient Fiancée
The Forgotten Gallo Bride
The Mistress That Tamed De Santis
The King's Captive Virgin

Available now!